Three Songs for Roxy

Conversation Pieces

A Small Paperback Series from Aqueduct Press

Subscriptions available: www.aqueductpress.com

1. The Grand Conversation
   Essays by L. Timmel Duchamp
2. With Her Body
   Short Fiction by Nicola Griffith
3. Changeling
   A Novella by Nancy Jane Moore
4. Counting on Wildflowers
   An Entanglement by Kim Antieau
5. The Traveling Tide
   Short Fiction by Rosaleen Love
6. The Adventures of the Faithful Counselor
   A Narrative Poem by Anne Sheldon
7. Ordinary People
   A Collection by Eleanor Arnason
8. Writing the Other
   A Practical Approach
   by Nisi Shawl & Cynthia Ward
9. Alien Bootlegger
   A Novella by Rebecca Ore
10. The Red Rose Rages (Bleeding)
    A Short Novel by L. Timmel Duchamp
11. Talking Back: Epistolary Fantasies
    edited by L. Timmel Duchamp
12. Absolute Uncertainty
    Short Fiction by Lucy Sussex
13. Candle in a Bottle
    A Novella by Carolyn Ives Gilman

14. Knots
    Short Fiction by Wendy Walker

15. Naomi Mitchison: A Profile of Her Life and Work
    A Monograph by Lesley A. Hall

16. We, Robots
    A Novella by Sue Lange

17. Making Love in Madrid
    A Novella by Kimberly Todd Wade

18. Of Love and Other Monsters
    A Novella by Vandana Singh

19. Aliens of the Heart
    Short Fiction by Carolyn Ives Gilman

20. Voices From Fairyland:
    The Fantastical Poems of Mary Coleridge, Charlotte Mew, and Sylvia Townsend Warner
    Edited and With Poems by Theodora Goss

21. My Death
    A Novella by Lisa Tuttle

22. De Secretis Mulierum
    A Novella by L. Timmel Duchamp

23. Distances
    A Novella by Vandana Singh

24. Three Observations and a Dialogue:
    Round and About SF
    Essays by Sylvia Kelso and a correspondence with Lois McMaster Bujold

25. The Buonarotti Quartet
    Short Fiction by Gwyneth Jones

26. Slightly Behind and to the Left
    Four Stories & Three Drabbles by Claire Light

27. Through the Drowsy Dark
    Short Fiction and Poetry by Rachel Swirsky

28. Shotgun Lullabies
    Stories and Poems by Sheree Renée Thomas

29. A Brood of Foxes
    A Novella by Kristin Livdahl
30. The Bone Spindle
    Poems and Short Fiction by Anne Sheldon
31. The Last Letter
    A Novella by Fiona Lehn
32. We Wuz Pushed
    On Joanna Russ and Radical Truth-Telling
    by Brit Mandelo
33. The Receptionist and Other Tales
    Poems by Lesley Wheeler
34. Birds and Birthdays
    Stories by Christopher Barzak
35. The Queen, the Cambion, and Seven Others
    Stories by Richard Bowes
36. Spring in Geneva
    A Novella by Sylvia Kelso
37. The XY Conspiracy
    A Novella by Lori Selke
38. Numa
    An Epic Poem
    by Katrinka Moore
39. Myths, Metaphors, and Science Fiction:
    Ancient Roots of the Literature of the Future
    Essays by Sheila Finch
40. NoFood
    Short Fiction by Sarah Tolmie
41. The Haunted Girl
    Poetry and Short Stories by Lisa M. Bradley
42. Three Songs for Roxy
    A Novella by Caren Gussoff
43. Ghost Signs
    Poems and a Short Story by Sonya Taaffe

44. The Prince of the Aquamarines & The Invisible Prince: Two Fairy Tales
    by Louise Cavelier Levesque
45. Back, Belly, and Side: True Lies and False Tales
    Short Fiction by Celeste Rita Baker
46. A Day in Deep Freeze
    A Novella by Lisa Shapter
47. A Field Guide to the Spirits
    Poems by Jean LeBlanc
48. Marginalia to Stone Bird
    Poems by Rose Lemberg
49. Unpronounceable
    A Novella by Susan diRende
50. Sleeping Under the Tree of Life
    Poetry and Short Fiction by Sheree Renée Thomas
51. Other Places
    Short Fiction by Karen Heuler
52. Monteverde: Memoirs of an Interstellar Linguist
    A Novella by Lola Robles,
    translated by Lawrence Schimel
53. The Adventure of the Incognita Countess
    A Novella by Cynthia Ward
54. Boundaries, Border Crossings, and Reinventing the Future
    Essays and Short Fiction by Beth Plutchak
55. Liberating the Astronauts
    Poems by Christina Rau
56. In Search of Lost Time
    A Novella by Karen Heuler

About the Aqueduct Press Conversation Pieces Series

The feminist engaged with sf is passionately interested in challenging the way things are, passionately determined to understand how everything works. It is my constant sense of our feminist-sf present as a grand conversation that enables me to trace its existence into the past and from there see its trajectory extending into our future. A genealogy for feminist sf would not constitute a chart depicting direct lineages but would offer us an ever-shifting, fluid mosaic, the individual tiles of which we will probably only ever partially access. What could be more in the spirit of feminist sf than to conceptualize a genealogy that explicitly manifests our own communities across not only space but also time?

Aqueduct's small paperback series, Conversation Pieces, aims to both document and facilitate the "grand conversation." The Conversation Pieces series presents a wide variety of texts, including short fiction (which may not always be sf and may not necessarily even be feminist), essays, speeches, manifestoes, poetry, interviews, correspondence, and group discussions. Many of the texts are reprinted material, but some are new. The grand conversation reaches at least as far back as Mary Shelley and extends, in our speculations and visions, into the continually-created future. In Jonathan Goldberg's words, "To look forward to the history that will be, one must look at and retell the history that has been told." And that is what Conversation Pieces is all about.

L. Timmel Duchamp

Jonathan Goldberg, "The History That Will Be" in Louise Fradenburg and Carla Freccero, eds., *Premodern Sexualities* (New York and London: Routledge, 1996)

Published by Aqueduct Press
PO Box 95787
Seattle, WA 98145-2787
www.aqueductpress.com

ISBN: 978-1-61976-073-8

A slightly different version of "Free Bird" appeared in *Bloodchildren: Stories by the Octavia E. Butler Scholars*, edited by Nisi Shawl, Carl Brandon Society, 2013.

Original Block Print of Mary Shelley by Justin Kempton:
www.writersmugs.com

Conversation Pieces
Volume 42

Three Songs for Roxy

by
Caren Gussoff

For Christopher, as they all are and will be.

Nayís tuke to Cat Rambo and Nisi Shawl, for reading, editing, and cheerleading; Wayward Café, for their unceasing hospitality and patronage of Seattle SFF; Timmi Duchamp for her encouragement, tireless editing, and faith in the work; and the *Rrom* writers and activists I have connected with online and in person, for their support and warmth.

A note on language: I used words and phrases from the *Kalderash* dialect, a subset of *Vlax Romani*. While the *Kalderash* may be found world-wide, they are just one of the families of the *Rrom* people. If you'd like to learn more about the *Rrom* people today, the International Romani Union (http://internationalromaniunion.org/home-en/) is a good place to start.

Contents

s

Part One: Free Bird

Káko Fatlip's third wedding was the day after my sister Roxy's twenty-first birthday. So she begged and pleaded with our parents to let us drive to Florida together instead of both of us going with the caravan.

Mamo wanted to say no; our mother wanted us all together when we traveled. But right after we returned from the wedding, Tate had a *chav* from San Bernardino coming to look over Roxy. Mamo and Tate said he was coming to meet both of us, but he wasn't, and we all knew it. Besides, Roxy had a talent for whining, especially when she had an indisputable point: it could be the last time I spend any time with Kizzy before one of us becomes a *bori*, and then we'd be planning her wedding, and then she'd be pregnant and it'd never be the same.

Really, Roxy just wanted to spend a few days drinking and dancing inside the honky tonks in Large Head and Sweet Tea before everyone started arriving and we had to spend a week in ankle-skimming *tsóxa* playing good gypsy girls in front of the whole family.

Tate and Mamo knew it, too. But Roxy and I were really close, and our parents considered me as good a chaperone as any brother or father. So, Tate changed the oil and rotated the tires on the blue pickup, and I was off to get Roxy and then to Florida.

It was a two-hour drive south and into the Klamath to the fire station. Roxy'd been working as a wildfire lookout since May, and we'd spoken only a few times, although she emailed me nearly every night, short bits of nothing, about the stars or the boredom, the heat or the rain.

Roxy was waiting for me by the trail head. She'd cropped her hair, and was brown from the sun and sharply thin, but when she threw herself into my arms, she felt fit and taut as a working dog.

"*Rovli*!" she yelled and kissed me. I hated when she used my nickname, "Stick." But I knew how she meant it, with love. She dragged me by my arm and introduced me to the other hotshots. "This is my sister, Kizzy," she said. Each one had a name like a superhero and shook my hand vigorously, even though they had to look up. Maybe because they had to look up.

"Are you a model?" one asked. Another asked me if I played basketball.

"Neither," I answered. As always, it sounded like a bit of an apology.

Afterward, Roxy shot me secret sister signals about this one or that, whooping a hand over her mouth at the handsome ones, tipping her wrist behind the ones that couldn't hold their liquor.

We ate a dinner of ham and eggs and talked excitedly, as if we weren't about to spend three days and nights on the road together, driving straight through/. Roxy admired my shoes and my sweater—both new, both from my job at Macy's, bought on sale and with my associate discount—and I ran a hand through her spiky hair. It looked wet but felt dry. "It fits better under the helmet," she explained.

As we helped with the dishes, the hotshots grunted and seemed like they would genuinely miss my sister whom they described to me as a "natural" and "a lot of fun." They seemed not to know what to make of me, so they made conversation telling me kind things about Roxy. They'd miss her, they said, and knowing Roxy, I believed them. They all made a show of helping us into the truck, and we let them.

Roxy waved at her co-workers and jumped into the driver's seat. She swung her legs for leverage as she adjusted the driver's seat. "I'll drive us out of here," she said. "I know this country backwards now."

There was nothing to it, really, just a mile back onto the gravel road, then the old macadam, then asphalt, then the highway. But Roxy bounced behind the wheel, so I returned to the passenger's seat.

"Where shall we go?" Roxy asked. "Toronto? Acapulco? New York City?" and smacked the seat between us. "I feel good. I feel lucky, *baXtali,*" she said, adjusting the rear view mirror and shoving the truck into gear. "*Po drom,*" she said, pumping a fist as the wheels kicked up black dirt. "Let's go."

Mamo had strong ideas about *baXt*, luck. Finding a coin minted in one of our birth years was lucky. Picking up a rock with a hole in it was lucky. Seeing a butterfly was lucky. Carrying a packet of salt in your purse was lucky. Catching a falling leaf was lucky. Listing lucky things was lucky.

Feeling lucky was lucky.

And, as my mother would sit and watch natural disasters unfold on the television, footage of the hills outside Austin on fire, earthquakes cracking the Washington monument, major river floods in the Upper Midwest, and hurricanes pounding the Gulf, she would reiterate how I, her foundling daughter, was the luckiest of all.

"We could be any of those places," she'd say. "But we aren't." She'd reach out to touch me or stroke my hair, and if she couldn't reach me, just hold her palm in my direction. "Our road luck finds us here."

Meaning that instead of chasing *baXt po drom*, luck on the road, like the rest of the Gypsies, Mamo and Tate and Roxy—and, by choice, Mamo's brother Marko, his wife Gracie, and grandma Olive Dei—were tied here. In one place. To the trailers rusting a ring into the ground behind the façade, propped against the converted mother-in-law house that Mamo and Aunt Gracie split right down the middle as an *ofisa*—one-half for Mamo's life coaching business and one-half for Gracie's fortune-telling parlor.

My family didn't want to take the chance that if my people came looking for me, when they inevitably realized their mistake in leaving me behind, they wouldn't be able to find me on the road like *Rrom* find each other.

"If you'd been *gadjo*," Dei told me, "we wouldn't care. They throw away everything. But your people lent you to us for a reason. They saw how we are for our children, and that's why they trust us with something so precious and beautiful."

It was love that kept them there, a few blocks from where they found me. There were other reasons, equally important but less primary: no one knew exactly what I was or what I would become. My insides were not exactly as expected, and my family couldn't risk me becoming sick or hurt. It took a complex, carefully-cultivated relationship with Stanley Levowitz, MD's superstitious and co-dependent wife Elizabeth Denny Peabody Levowitz, involving the best of both Mamo and Gracie's trade delivered to Elizabeth weekly, that got me medical care well under the radar of universities, research labs, and the government. *BaXtali*, Mamo said of Elizabeth's addiction to spiritual advisement and Stanley's deep embarrassment for his wife's mental frailties; he wouldn't tell if we didn't. So far, he hadn't.

I was also a complicated victory for Mamo. She wanted her children to have an education, stability, choices, easier with a permanent address. That meant less traveling, no matter how you did the math.

And I was a perfect excuse, a reasonable explanation, a water-tight alibi to put down roots that made her look good no matter which way it was told. She wanted her daughters to straddle worlds, between *Rrom* and *gadjo*. And if luck would have it that one of her daughters was between two worlds, that was how it should be.

And so, anytime we got to travel was doubly exciting, fraught with danger and intrigue. That was why Mamo had wanted the whole family to travel together instead of letting us two girls go alone. But Mamo knew Roxy was right when she said this would be the last time we could be together like this. Even if Roxy didn't marry this *chav*—although Tate was pulling hard for him, from a real *Rrom baro* California family—she'd marry the next one, or the one after that. And even though Mamo hated the idea of me outside the perimeter of the five miles around the trailers and suspected that we were aiming to do some carousing or some such no good, she maintained the delicate veneer of deniability and approved the trip.

Roxy drove into the deep orange like she could outrun twilight. I crossed my arms and stared meaningfully at the speedometer, like the dutiful big sister. Roxy, like the naughty little sister, ignored my staring.

"I've got music," Roxy said, like that was what we'd been talking about, and reached behind the seat where she'd stashed her tote bag. She held onto the wheel with one hand and steered with the other, bouncing the truck like a boat close to shipwreck. I grabbed the wheel as Roxy pulled out a CD and shoved it into the stereo. "A friend made me this CD."

I started to curse out my sister and her driving, but Free Bird started and she turned up the volume to preemptively drown me out. "I love this song," she shouted and sang along loudly: "When I cleave your face tomorrow, will you dismember me?"

It had the desired effect. I stopped staring at the speed and laughed at my sister. To reciprocate, she slowed down the truck a bit. "And Candace Bergen cannot cha-a-a-ange." Roxy slapped the steering wheel and held her face in a wolf howl as she sang.

But we grew silent when the song slid into its five-minute outro, and then into a love song I didn't recognize. I glanced at my sister and scratched my little finger. "A friend made this for you?"

Roxy didn't answer that, but she clicked the volume down a few bars, just low enough to talk. "So," she said. "What do you know about the *chav* from Barstow Tate's importing to sniff at us?"

I couldn't tell if I had made my finger itch by scratching it, or if I had just noticed that it was itching. I licked my finger and wiped it on my pants. "I don't know much."

"Tate will have one of us married off yet." She glanced at me, as if there was a question which one of us it would be. "I don't want—" Then she glanced at me again. "Are you scratching?"

"No," I said. "Maybe. No. Definitely not." I was. "Do you have any lotion on you?"

"In my bag," Roxy answered, and started to turn around to get behind her seat.

I grabbed her arm. "I'll get it." I pulled the bag onto my knees. Inside was a tumble of papers and a scarf that let out puffs of perfume when I moved it. Toward the bottom was a tube of cocoa butter. I rubbed some onto my hands. It stung.

It was starting. I wanted to scream.

The next exit had a truck stop and diner at the bottom of the off-ramp. Roxy flicked the directional signal. We pulled up to the pumps, and in the fluorescent light my hand looked as pink as the ham we had for dinner.

"Fuck," Roxy said. She looked at me briefly, concerned for my feelings, and then said it again.

"I can probably make it," I said.

"Fuck." Roxy sighed a few times. "No. You'll be miserable, and I will be miserable that you are miserable." She leaned down to her bag, gathered at my feet. "You want to call Mamo, or should I?"

I looked at my hands. "I can take a bus home."

"Don't be stupid, *Rovli*." Roxy sighed again, then put on a brave face. "Go get ice. I'll call Mamo." She reached for me, but I had the door open, feet on the ground. "It's OK, Kiz. It really is."

"No," I said. "It isn't."

Roxy pulled her phone from the depths of her bag. "It will be."

Some stories aren't meant to be told. The more they get told, the more they change from what they once were, worn down and smooth like pieces of sea glass too beautiful to have ever been broken bottles. In the telling, mundane stories become colorful, colorful becomes fantastic, fantastic becomes legend, and legend becomes myth. Some stories aren't meant to be beautiful or mythic, they are meant to be true—*chachi paramicha*—and so those are better not told.

Mamo can tell me every detail up to and after finding me. It was too humid for Seattle, and the rains wouldn't come. Lake Union smelled like swamp gas instead of salt and fish. She was seven months pregnant with Roxy, who had settled right on her bladder. She and Tate had made it out of the trailer and into the truck when she had to go to the bathroom. She wouldn't make it back to the *trela*, and Gracie had a client in the office. So she waddled next door to the empty lot to squat. The lot was empty, had been empty for years, with green, plenty of private areas to let loose behind the support beams that held up the Interstate.

Mamo ran toward a beam, but then she saw me and called for Tate. After that, she said, her memories are fuzzy, like she was very drunk or dreaming. I was lying on a rock under a tree, she said, sleeping soundly and shimmering as if I were wet. My legs were too long, stiff and loose like bell clappers when she picked me up. But I opened my eyes and wrapped my arms around her like I was much older than the three months she estimated I had to be, and from that moment, she says, I was theirs.

She doesn't remember whether she even went and peed.

I once asked Uncle Marko, who had the best memory in the family, for details. "I don't know, Kizzy. When they brought you home, you didn't look like anything."

"Like anything?"

"Like an infant, I guess. But you seemed, blurry. You were so quiet. And long. That was odd. I don't know. It took a few days before you seemed real." Then he shook his head.

I often waded through the blackberry brambles, looking for clues. The lot is still empty, the weeping maple thick and fragrant, the rock carpeted with a quilt of moss and mold and mushrooms thickly obscuring anything that could have told me anything.

I peeled for the first time when I was five. It started on my hands and feet. We hadn't yet developed our affiliation with Elizabeth Denny Peabody Levowitz, so Mamo was left to her own diagnostic devices. She immediately ruled out a burn or chicken pox; she knew those well. She hit the internet for articles about allergies, rashes, and eczema, as long scales of silvery skin peeled away from me in sheets to reveal shiny pink beneath. My mother soaked me in oatmeal baths, rubbed olive oil into my skin, put me in the sun, protected me from the sun, and decided, after looking long and hard at hundreds of photos of skin diseases, that I had plaque psoriasis.

Tate watched me rub my back against the garden wall like a molting snake against rock, and said, "She doesn't have soreitis, Mala. She's—" He didn't finish his sentence because he caught me looking at him, stopped cold in the middle of a scratch.

He'd say this same thing many times throughout my life. "She's…" and usually end by saying "…my girl" and hug me in his hairy arms. And that moment, he said, "She's fine," and went over and picked me up, flipped me onto my tummy and rubbed at my itchy skin with his beard until I laughed with relief.

Later, I knew what he'd been going to say, each time. *Alien. She's an alien, Mala, doing whatever aliens do.* But he never said it. Not once when I could hear, and probably not ever.

He loved me. But also, there is no real Romany word for alien. There are only a few words for anyone not Rrom—*gadjo*, white person, *rakli*, non-gypsy kid, *streyino*, stranger. *Djuli*, American. But I've never heard a word that means someone not entirely—or at all—human.

My psoriasis, whether or not it was psoriasis, was one of my more convincingly human quirks. It was as if I was built by someone who'd read about humans, but never actually seen one. My growth spurts left me nearly seven feet tall. I had pores but never a blemish or a pimple. My hair was naturally shiny but all one flat color, like a cheap dye job. My toes and fingers were all the same length. And I had no lines across my palms.

This most disturbed my Aunt Gracie the most. Mamo respected Aunt Gracie's profession not because there was any credence to it, above and beyond the cultural tradition of it, the encyclopedic knowledge of human nature one had to have to be successful, and the fact that Gracie could literally itemize the long gold earrings she wore and the thousands of scarves she draped and tied all over her half of the *ofisa*. But, Mamo said, her *phen* had started to believe her own shit.

Dei tried to put the whole issue of my palms to bed one family dinner, looking up suddenly after one bite of her meatloaf and announcing that my palms were blank canvases upon which only I would carve the story of my life. "And we should all respect that," she finished, looking at Gracie.

A bag of ice was two dollars, and it'd last me until we got back home. I could lay my hand in it, then my arm, then my other hand and arm, and spare Roxy my fidgeting and moaning during the trip back to Seattle. I also bought Roxy two extra-big packs of peanut butter cups and a liter of iced tea, part as apology and part to keep her awake enough to drive.

By the pumps, Roxy was talking quietly into her phone and something about the way she slid her foot back and forth over a loose rock and shielded her face told me she wasn't speaking to our parents and not to ask questions. Her short hair stood up in electrified little spikes that made her look extra pretty and a little sad.

I slid over in the passenger seat and arranged the candy and tea on her seat, each one at a right angle to the other. I waited for her to be done.

When she opened the door, she glanced at the seat and smiled. "Thank you," she said, then placed them between our seats. She passed me the phone as she climbed in. "Call Mamo. I haven't yet."

I waited until we'd merged going north and dialed home. Mamo answered, the television blaring as it did every evening until Dei fell asleep, and she knew immediately as soon as I said hello.

"None of us will go," she said. "We will stay here. It's a bad omen anyway."

"Ma," I said, "I'll be fine. You all should go. And take Roxy down too. I'm fine; it's nothing different," and I was fine and it wasn't any different. I'd itch and peel, and then it would be over. My skin would be sensitive to lotion or perfume, and then it'd be another day. I didn't need care or an audience, and in fact would hide in my part of the trailer beneath a soft fleece blanket until it was done. Then I'd shake out the sheets and the blankets, and it'd be done. Until it happened again.

"We'll discuss it when you get home," she said, and after a bunch of kisses to Roxy and back and forth with everyone home, I hung up and opened the sack of ice at my feet. The cold felt great, and I watched the headlights of the cars heading south.

I would have fallen asleep but Roxy started singing again. "I've got to be traveling on now..." She turned to me, as if waiting for me to join in again, but when I didn't, she tapped her ear as if it were clogged. "Crap," she said. "That song. It gets in there, yeah?"

"It's called an ear worm." I leaned over and turned up the stereo, then pushed the back button until I heard the opening notes. "The only cure," I explained, and we sang and drove into the night.

Not too long after the first time I peeled, Mamo started telling Roxy and me the story of Lallah Pombo. She never told it the same way twice, yet it was always the same.

"There was and was not," she'd say, "in the long ago days, a gypsy family who found a young girl. They called her Lallah Pombo and took her back to their caravan, which never traveled. They raised Lallah and loved Lallah and Lallah was their very own. They all lived in peace and abundance and sang and danced for the sun and the moon and the rain, who together had raised them and loved them and made them their own.

"One day, the rain didn't come, even though the sun and the moon did. This happened for a long time. They sang for the rain, and they noticed Lallah couldn't sing on key. They danced for the rain, and they saw that Lallah couldn't keep a beat. They berated her and called her useless, but the only rain they saw came from Lallah's eyes."

Always, around this point in the story, Roxy knew nothing in the story was going to be about her, so she stopped listening and fell asleep.

Mamo would continue: "So, Lallah ran away to find the rain. She wandered to the city and she sat among scholars and merchants and laborers and adventurers, but no one knew where the rain lived. She wandered from village to village to city to city, and the only rain came from her eyes.

"One day, she reached the end of the world, at the shore of a great sea. The sun and the moon both shone down, and she knew she had found the rain. The rain appeared to her and asked why the gypsies sent her.

"I am useless, she answered. I cannot sing, and I cannot dance, and I have nothing else to give my people.

"The rain patted her shoulders and soaked her hair and spread across the lands. But first he told her, You have found me and are not useless. You will go home and you will tell the stories of what you have seen. Then your people will travel, and sing and dance the stories for everyone all over the world. And wherever you go, I will follow and the land will give you all that you need."

One night, Mamo tucked us in and told us the story. Roxy was asleep by the middle, as she always was, but when Mamo was finished, she tucked a stuffed elephant toy under Roxy's heavy arm, and a stuffed unicorn toy under mine.

Roxy rolled onto her new elephant and snored quietly. Mamo watched as I turned the unicorn around and around in my hands. "Do you know what it is?" she asked. "It's a magical animal. A unicorn. Very special. Just like you." Then she flicked off the lamp, kissed me, then Roxy, and left our trailer.

I lay in the dark, that night, for a long time. Then I pulled out a flashlight and my sewing box. I ripped the unicorn's horn off and carefully pinned the wound closed with tiny safety pins from a sewing kit.

Mamo never commented when she saw me lugging it around the next day, her Lallah Pombo and a plain old stuffed horse.

She never stopped telling the story.

Our home looked like any other house, from the outside, although it seemed suspiciously close to the tiny neighboring house that held the *ofisa.* When they were newlyweds, Tate had found a three-quarter house façade behind a movie studio. It was the whole front, complete with a functioning Cape Cod front door. If you asked them how they trucked the thing over a thousand miles, Tate and Mamo hooded their eyes with mischief. "In pieces," Mamo would say, "Whole and tied to the top," Tate would say. But they got it back to Seattle in more or less one piece and propped the thing up, next to the mother-in-law house, the backside secured down with sandbags.

Roxy and I spent many hours debating whether it was more or less humiliating that we had the front and side of a house, but no back.

You could walk around the left side or behind the *ofisa* to get to the trailers, but Mamo liked us to use that Cape Cod door, which opened to her gardens and the hot tub set in front of the trailers. It was something like a miracle Mamo got anything to grow at all under the shade of the freeway, and she supplemented what wouldn't flourish in the few slants of light with plastic flowers. She and Dei would water the real and fake plants equally, and spray them all with sugar water to the delight and confusion of bees and butterflies.

The truck came to a stop and shut off, and I woke with a start, arms to the elbows deep in the bag of melting ice.

"We're here, Kiz," Roxy said. "Wake up."

Aunt Gracie and Uncle Marko were either fighting, or Marko had been drinking hard liquor and was snoring, because she emerged from the *ofisa* to greet us. She hugged Roxy tight against her kimono, and then hugged me equally, as if she hadn't seen me all summer as well.

"Were you trying to call?" Gracie asked us. "The phone kept ringing, and no one was there."

We shook our heads.

"Well, then, go on inside," she said to us. "Mala won't sleep until she sees you." She pulled a cigarette from inside a voluminous sleeve. "I'm not sleeping either, but that's because your *Káko* wants to kill me with his snoring." She lit the cigarette, then shooed us. "Go on."

Roxy went first, through the red door and over to our parents' trailer. I went straight to our trailer, kicked off my shoes and wrapped myself in my fleece blanket.

Roxy came in and dumped her bag across her half of the back room. I pretended to be asleep. She tiptoed out, but through the open window I could hear her on her phone.

"Are you sure?" she asked. "I'm sure. I just want to make sure—" Silence. Then, "My sister will be here." Quiet. "I want to tell Kizzy. She's the only one—" Hush. "The train is lovely." A pause. "Phone me with your info. Of course I'll pick you up." Footsteps.

She was back in the trailer. She dropped her clothes on the floor and ran a shower. Now, all I could hear was Uncle Marko's honking, slightly muffled. Roxy stepped out, and the trailer filled with the smell of artificial vanilla.

"Kizzy? I know you're awake."

I answered her a noise, like "Ungh."

She waited, as if I would say more. I heard her plug in something, then rub her wet head with the towel.

She slipped into her bed. "I love you, *Rovli,*" she said, then music filled her earphones. I lay awake through two complete repeats of the CD, Free Bird to Free Bird before I fell asleep.

I'd always hoped the peeling would reveal itself to be cyclical somehow, predictable like menstruation, or have some sort of triggers I could avoid, like hot foods or wheat gluten. Instead, it seemed to come and go as it pleased, lasting two, three days, leaving me clean and raw.

Mamo used peeling as fertile testing grounds for the motivational techniques she employed in her life coaching. I could never stay home or beg out of events. If I could stand, she said, I could run, and if I could run, I could fly. If I could fly, then I could go to school.

Tate would roll his eyes. He'd sometimes push Mamo to let me stay home, and Mamo would consent but let us know she considered it a defeat. "Your Tate," she'd say, "is too old-fashioned when it comes to girls. He's afraid of attracting too much attention." She'd sigh here, for emphasis. "He doesn't understand we're Americans."

But Mamo was as old-fashioned as Tate when it came to marriage. She expected it of us, like she expected us to eat and to sleep and shit and be happy and cry. Not marrying was as implausible as denying death.

Granted, she wanted us to have some autonomy regarding our husbands, to even like them. Her own marriage was *baXtali*, considering that Uncle Fatlip, then sixteen but already the man of the family, acted on her behalf and accepted the first offer for her. Uncle Fatlip did well, accidentally, so Mamo couldn't hold onto any bad feelings toward her brother, even when he spent her *bori* price on his own first two marriages. But Mamo leaned hard on Tate to wait for offers until we turned, at least, twenty-one.

And now we were.

Mamo gently squeezed my shoulder until I awoke. "How is it?"

"*Na dara*, Ma. I'm fine."

"I should be staying with you," she said, and I realized she was already in her traveling clothes, scarf holding back her long hair.

The past two days had been a fever dream of itch and fatigue. "I've peeled. It's done," I said. "Besides, Fatlip is your brother. You have to go."

"We could have girls' time. The three of us," she began, then sighed, resigned. "At least you two will get good time together."

"Roxy's staying?"

"Roxy's staying." Mamo laid a stack of cash on my side table. "This should be plenty. Use some to get her a birthday cake from Borrachini's? And a bottle of wine?"

"I will."

"And something nice? From your job?"

I nodded.

"And if it gets worse, you'll call Levowitz?"

"I promise."

As Mamo hugged me, the phone rang. Mamo pulled back, and answered our extension. She just held the phone to her ear without saying anything.

"What—" but she shushed me with a finger. After a few seconds, she simply hung up.

"Someone," she said, "just keeps calling. They don't say anything, but I can hear them. Do you think it's something bad? A creeper? Should we stay here?"

Then Tate came in. "It's a wrong number, I tell you," he said. "Or a bill collector." He smiled at that, but Mamo did not.

Tate came over and ruffled my hair. "We should head out, Mala."

"All right," Mamo said. "But you girls keep the doors locked. Just in case."

Then Tate kissed me and Mamo kissed me, and I waddled stiffly out of bed to wave to Dei, Gracie, and *Káko* Marko. Roxy and I stood side by side as they drove away.

The hot tub was a gift from Uncle Marko. *Káko* was a trader by occupation. By passion. He was continually up-swapping something for something else: car parts for a flat of soymilk, a flat of soymilk for a collection of old Playboys, a Playboy collection for a pinball machine. Occasionally, when he up-traded to something valuable enough, he would sell it.

Káko kept a photo of a Canadian *gadjo* in his wallet. He'd pull it out as motivation. The kid had traded a single paperclip for a house in Saskatchewan. *One red paperclip*, he'd say, with great reverence.

Marko might have been able to trade that hot tub up for something, or even sell it. But instead, he traded again, for a couple of hours from a pair of sad-faced apprentice plumbers to install the tub in the center of the garden. He said it was for everyone, but looked at me when he demonstrated how it worked. Trailer showers gave me cramps from stooping.

No one else ever really used it. Dei tried it twice to ease her arthritis, deemed it "excellent," and then never used it again. Gracie would use it to work out neck cricks if she had to spend a few nights on the *ofisa* sofa, but that was rare. I liked to use it at night, after everyone else had retired into their trailers and wasn't passing by, averting their eyes in simulated privacy. Besides, if it was a very dark, clear night, if I hung my head back, I could see a few stars in the strip of sky between the overpasses.

I uncovered the tub and slipped in. Even over the hum of the jets, I could hear music from our trailer. "Roxy, not that CD again," I said toward the glow of her laptop.

"I love this CD," she called back.

I let the warm water clear off the last of the loose skin, sticky and fine as cobwebs. My skin had finished its peeling, and I thought about calling in to pick up a morning shift at work, then getting Roxy a cake and bringing home Chinese. Then Roxy turned down the music. I heard her say, "Hello," then "No, this is her sister," and then, again, "Hello?" A moment later, she came out of the trailer. "Someone just called and asked for you," she said. "Then they hung up."

"Who was it?"

"No idea. It was male, though," she said, and waggled her eyebrows.

"Har," I answered. It must have been the silent caller again, and Roxy thought she was being funny.

She sat up on the side of the tub to talk to me.

"I was reading up on ear worms," she said, letting her bare feet dangle in the water. "Scientists aren't sure what causes them."

"I'm pretty sure repetition has something to do with it," I answered.

She splashed me in response. "A friend made me that CD."

"So you said." I looked at my beautiful sister in the darkness, the shape of her nose, her thin, muscled arms, the curve of her breasts, and I drew up my knees, light green in the trailer light reflecting off the water, and large as cabbages. I wondered which *chav* sent her the CD, if it was the one Tate had coming, or if it was another. Someone was going to love my sister very soon, and I felt protective of her. I wanted to hold the back of her head in my hand. I had an unexplainable, sick, nostalgic feeling about everything. As things happened, they were already gone.

But instead, I straightened my legs and watched the sky. My sister kicked her feet gently in the tub.

"Ever wish Mamo and Tate would let us date who we want?" Roxy asked quietly.

"I never thought about it."

"Really?" Roxy asked. "I think about it a lot." Her feet bobbed around like elegant fish. "About picking your own—" she paused, searching for the word, "—mate." She leaned down, as if to brush something from her calf, then continued. "Like, what if I brought home someone white? Or Chinese? Or Jewish?"

"Is your CD-making friend white, Chinese, or Jewish?"

Roxy ignored that. "I mean, how hard would they freak out? How much would they hate me?" she asked. Her tone suggested she already knew the answer.

It was a new moon, and the sky was dark. If I squinted, then I could ignore the smoky haze of headlights on the freeway.

"There's something I want to tell you," Roxy said.

But then, a flash, a blaze across the sky. "A shooting star," I said, and Roxy craned her neck. We watched the bright pink ionization trail until it disappeared behind the southbound lanes.

"That's lucky," she said.

"Make a wish," I told her.

When exactly does waiting stop? What does it take before expectation, hope, and dread become just another day, and just another day becomes your life?

How long can we stay ever-vigilant before we slacken and relax? And that for which we have spent our life preparing for becomes a surprise—a car crash or a punch in the jaw. We know what to do. We've worked it out, imagined it, but then find ourselves utterly cold: why?

The preparation becomes itself a story. Colorful, fantastic, legend, myth, and distant as a shooting star. Beautiful, miraculous, *baXtali*, but nothing more.

In retrospect, I paid attention to all the wrong things. I relaxed. I made assumptions.

We're only human.

Roxy poked me awake. I opened my eyes, and she was leaning over me.

"Kizzy," she said. "I have to talk to you." She sat down on the floor next to my bed, cross-legged, and balanced her phone in one hand. She waited for me to sit up, encouraging me to hurry by staring.

"Is everything OK?" I asked. I couldn't remember the last time Roxy voluntarily woke up before I did; then again, she'd just spent a summer working crazy, long shifts, watching and wandering the deep forests of Oregon.

"*Na dara*," she said. "I just have to tell you."

"OK."

Roxy opened and closed her mouth, thinking, like she did sometimes when she had to use only English or only Romany, and had to plan her words carefully. Then she said it. "I'm a lesbian."

The words hung like dust in the air. She expected a reaction. The only one I could give her was, "So?"

She sat up on the bed, then leaned into me, wrapped her arms around me. She sobbed in my shoulder, partly happy, partly miserable.

"So?" I repeated.

She didn't answer, just lay on my nightshirt, wet with tears and snot. She calmed down, then sat back and looked at me.

"Did you wonder why we drove straight south from the fire station?"

"Not really."

"I was going to tell you on the road. I didn't want to go to Sweet Tea or Large Head. I wanted to go to Oakland."

"California?"

"Yeah," she said.

"To see your friend. The one that made you the CD. The white, Chinese, Jewish one."

"Yeah." Roxy sniffed. "I don't think she is Chinese or Jewish, though."

"And I messed up the plans."

"It's OK, *Rovli.* You didn't mess up anything. She's coming here instead. Her train gets in soon." Roxy looked at her phone. "An hour. She's going to stay a few days."

"OK."

"You're really OK with this?"

"Why wouldn't I be?" I swung my legs over the side of the bed and stretched them.

"Tate and Mamo won't be. This is going to kill them. They are going to kill me." She put her head in her hands. "You don't understand."

It annoyed me that she thought I didn't understand. Our parents loved me, and they found me under a tree. I started to shake my head, but Roxy started talking again. "You went to bed," she said. "They yelled at me for two hours about cutting my hair before that *chav* comes."

"Your hair was pretty," I said, trying to explain, but she shot me a look.

"He's coming for me," she said. We stared at each other, the shock of the truth a palatable thing. This was something we all knew, but we never said these things, just like no one ever said what I was. Saying it out loud made Roxy bolder and look sadder. "I think they already made the deal," she said. "I think they already took my *bori* price."

"Mamo would never—"

"Oh, Kiz, don't be stupid," Roxy said. "It's different for you." She remembered my feelings and scanned my face. She grabbed my foot and squeezed it. "I'd trade places with you in a second."

I wanted to hide. Under the covers, my cabbage knees to my chest, my lineless hands over my smooth, shiny face. But I didn't. And couldn't. A girl my size hiding was even more ridiculous than the idea that a *chav* would choose me over my sister. That our parents would offer me up as a bride. "What's her name?" I asked. "You'd better get going to pick up—"

"Natalie." Roxy's mouth smiled when she said it, even though the rest of her looked pinched, panicked.

"Natalie," I repeated. "I won't tell Mamo and Tate. But you will have to."

Roxy looked at me again, this time as if she wished I would hold the back of her head in my hand and protect her.

"I'll be back," she said and stood up to go. She smoothed down her pants and ran one hand through her hair.

"Roxy," I called, but she was already gone. I got out of bed and put on some sweats and a tee-shirt to clean up before they returned. I wound up emptying and scrubbing out the hot tub, replaying the conversation over and over in my head. *I'm a lesbian*, my sister said, and I answered *So? I'm a lesbian,* she repeated, and I asked, *So what? It's different for you,* she said. I scrubbed the tub until the ringing phone made me stop.

I could hear breathing on the other end of the line. "Whoever you are," I said, with a surprising amount of conviction, "stop fucking around." Then I hung up.

The hot tub shone in the lights from the trailer.

So what? Then I said it aloud. "So what? I'm an alien."

Roxy and Natalie tumbled over one another like puppies, trying to get ready. I'd tried to leave the trailer three times, but each time they whined at me, like somehow I was an integral part of the goings on, so I tried to make myself as small as I could on my bed. Occasionally, a piece of clothing would get flung my way as they were searching for this or that. I held up a lacy thong that landed by my foot and flicked it back at them in an attempt to participate.

"You should come with us, *Rovli*," Roxy said into the mirror, threading earrings into her lobes.

"Please do," Natalie added.

They meant it, which was sweet. I wanted to say yes. I actually liked the club where they were going. It was dark and loud, and the booths were big enough to swallow even me up.

And I liked Natalie well enough. I could see why Roxy liked her; she was petite and blonde and easy with affection and always moving. In fact, it was hard to keep her in frame. She filled silences with unsteady laughs that were both strange and charming, and had a nervous habit of cracking her back. But not once did she stare at me or ask questions. Instead, when we met, she hugged me as high as she could reach, face in my stomach, and started talking as if we were in the middle of a conversation, started only moments before. As if we'd all known one another a long time.

I wanted to go. But when I opened my mouth to say yes, it came out as "No." *Yes.* My body wouldn't behave. My legs swung down, and my arms leaned into a drawer and extracted a bent paperback. "I'll stay here tonight." *Yes.* "You two have fun."

"Are you sure?" Roxy clicked her tongue, disappointed. "*Na dara,* you aren't in the way."

My head nodded. *No.* "I know."

Roxy flopped next to and on top of me while Natalie laced up her boots. "*Voliv tut.*"

"I love you, too," I said.

The taxi cab honked. The two of them hugged and petted me and then left in a cloud of glitter and perfume.

As the sun sank, the volume rose. Traffic roaring on the freeway overpass above, late summer cicadas hiding among the wax flowers in Mamo's garden. Even the lake seemed to have a sound, the air loud with smells, fishy salt, and tannins. I rolled open the trailer windows and lay back on my bunk, trying to read and half-hoping the phone would ring, then wishing it wouldn't.

I wandered around the bunk, straightening up, and padded outside to the *ofisa* to clear the sofa bed. Roxy hadn't said, but there was privacy in the *ofisa* and nowhere else. I turned on the portable television to keep me company, but no channels came in, even after two rescans of the digital converter box.

After I straightened up, I filled the clean hot tub and started the jets.

I tried not to feel sorry for myself. After all, I'd refused to go out with the girls. The tub filled, and I dropped my clothes there in the garden, acting as if the solitude was a gift. I sat in the tub and leaned back to look at the darkening, moonless sky, and when I was done, I dripped my way back to our trailer, dripped over the torrent of clothes, until I found a towel. I wrapped myself up and slid into my bed.

When I laid down my head, the noise stopped. The world stopped. It just stopped.

It started again with a great shake, then smaller ones, rattling the trailer like an empty can. I held on. Earthquake, I panicked. No, an accident on the freeway, just above, a semi breaking through steel guardrails. A tsunami. An explosion. A bomb, a solar flare. The switching of the magnetic poles. The apocalypse.

The trailer stopped shaking for a moment. Outside, the sky was darker than I'd ever seen. Then, shaking again, but this time, the air was what moved, thrumming and pulsing. I sucked in a breath and held it.

The air entered me like a demon, through my mouth. It was cold on my teeth, and as it traveled through me, my flesh jiggled separately from my bones. All my hair—head, neck, and arms—stood up. It smelled like magnetized iron. Thin, strong beams of lights poked through the open windows, searching like fingers.

I pushed out the breath I was holding. It came out loud and angry, a sound I'd never heard and wouldn't be able to reproduce. One blade of light found me, touched me, pulled me to my feet. I stood, naked, as the light traced over me. It was alive, I was sure, and its touch was one of a blind family friend marveling at how I'd grown.

I slapped it away.

The light hit the wall, and the trailer rocked like a dinghy in a storm. Outside, the truck's horn honked and the motor revved. I held on as best I could, but was tossed to my knees. I pulled myself toward the door as the trailer pitched to and fro, but before I could get there, something cold and dense whacked my arm.

A steel flashlight was suspended in mid-air. I reached for it, but it jumped against the ceiling with a *ding* and *clink* and clung there. More objects rose up, hovered—some necklaces of Roxy's, an underwire bra, a pocket knife—then jerked to the ceiling and the walls and just stuck there. *Ding, ding, ding,* loose change, earrings, my old stuffed unicorn, clinging by the pins holding its head together.

It felt like a vertical climb from my bed to the trailer door. But when I tumbled outside onto the ground, everything was oriented in the right direction: the ground was down, the trees grew up, and across the sky was the bottom of a spaceship.

The light blades searched for me again. I rolled into a ball and covered my head with my arms. The truck honked faster, revved harder, headlights flashing. Inside the trailer, Roxy's laptop switched on and off, blaring pieces of Free Bird through the speakers: "...leave here tomorrow...remember me...be traveling on... got to see..." The light found me, of course, stroked me gently in apology for frightening me. It ran through my hair and patted my shoulders, and, with magnetic fingers, tried to lift me up.

I didn't want to go. I stretched my full length and dug into the dirt and grass. I held onto my world. The light tried to pry me free, first softly, then in frustration. Mamo's flowers, wax and real, snapped at their stems.

We struggled, my mother and I. She was the light. The more it touched me, the more I felt her. The light scolded and begged, and I held on. The light pushed, rolled across the ground like water, unleashing sound and thunder that rained a shower of blunt safety glass.

"This is my home," I said or thought—it wasn't clear which—and the light gave a mother's sigh.

Then it was all over. They were gone for now, but they would be back. The truck's motor and headlights cut, and the ship was gone. The trailer clattered as everything again surrendered back to gravity.

Everything was still. No traffic or cicadas, no honking or Free Bird, a complete absence of sound except for my heart. The inside of my head felt bigger than the outside. I didn't move, didn't breathe. Rocks and glass and sharp plastic stems pushed sharply into my knees and hands, but I didn't dare do anything until the air settled back and the lights switched on, and even then I waited for the first brave cicada to tentatively chirp, for another to answer, for traffic noise and the lake waves hitting the shore. Only then did I exhale and sit down. By my foot was the stuffed unicorn, as if it'd followed me out of the trailer. It was dirty and a little damp, but I hugged it close as noises began trickling back.

I didn't know how long I sat there. Without the moon, it could have been minutes or hours. I sat and watched the path, willing Roxy to emerge from the darkness. I sat until the air condensed, beading on my skin. My teeth chattered, and I silenced them in the unicorn. Somewhere, inside one of the trailers, the phone rang three times in quick succession.

The footsteps were loud, crunching glass and twigs. Too heavy to be Roxy, but unmistakably human. Then, a silhouette, rectangular and male. Any other night and I probably would have been alarmed. But I was incapable of anything more than wiping my face on my unicorn, holding it as best as I could in front of my chest and calling out, "Hello?"

The silhouette stepped closer. He was in his thirties, with a square haircut but young eyes, which struggled to adjust in the low light. I saw him first, but it took me the full few seconds he needed to make me out to recognize him: Scott Lynn Miller, a loss prevention guard from the mall where I worked. It didn't make any sense that he was here. Before I could open my mouth, he came closer, asking if I was hurt.

"No," I answered. *Yes.* "What are you doing here, Scott Lynn Miller?"

Then he realized I was naked. "Ahhh," he started. He looked like he wanted to look, but he studied the ground. He held out his hand, still looking away. "I came looking for you."

Unthinking, I took his hand, but jerked away in surprise and pain. My hands were deeply cut and sticky. Scott Lynn Miller then grabbed my wrists and pulled me up. I swayed on my legs. I noticed his knuckles had a few strong black hairs on them.

"You're all wet," Scott Lynn Miller said. He kept his hand on my arm to steady me. He looked past me at the yard. "And everything's a mess." Then he made a surprised face at the ground. "I'm sorry," he said. "Is this how it always looks?"

I saw the garden, littered with broken glass and scattered belongings, my and Roxy's trailer nearly upended. "No," I said, a little annoyed and ashamed. "There was a—" I thought for a second, "—an earthquake."

It'd felt like an earthquake.

Scott Lynn Miller furrowed his brow until it almost reached his chin. "An earthquake?" He shook his head. "I didn't feel a thing." He looked around again, still not looking at me. "But it sure looks like an earthquake. Or Katrina." He looked back at me. "You know I was in Katrina, right?"

I did. It was one of the few things I did know about him. But I didn't really care. I was naked, I was cold and exhausted, and it didn't make any sense that he was there. "What are you doing here, Scott Lynn Miller?"

"You need to lie down," he said.

"That's my trailer," I answered, making a sloppy gesture to the upturned one, big enough to see in his peripheral vision.

"Whose are those?" he asked, jerking his chin at the others.

"My parents'. My aunt and uncle's and grandmother's."

"Are you alone?"

I started to nod, momentarily terrified. I didn't know why he was here. But then I remembered something else I knew about Scott Lynn Miller: he'd injured himself doing construction, and he was on a waiting list for the police academy. Which, I knew, did not in and of itself guarantee my safety in his presence, but there was also a freaking spaceship hovering above us somewhere containing my other, seemingly magnetic and destructive parents. "My sister's out with her girlfriend."

"Can you walk?" he asked, leading me a step towards my parent's trailer. I could, unsteady as a fawn. He led me, looking straight ahead at the door. He dropped my hand to push the door and looked away as I climbed the stairs, went inside, and fell onto Mamo and Tate's bed.

Inside, it looked like nothing had happened. A few things had rattled off their hooks or shelves, probably when our trailer tipped, and Scott Lynn Miller hung a frying pan back onto a hook and picked a book up from the floor. "An earthquake?" he asked again.

"An earthqu—" I answered, interrupting myself with a yawn. Scott Lynn Miller unfolded the comforter from the edge of the bed and covered me. This time, I was sure he looked, but my eyes were closing.

I dozed intermittently, feverishly, without dreaming. I listened for Roxy over the strange Scott Lynn Miller sounds: boiling water for tea, flipping through one of Mamo's self-help books, surfing through basic cable channels. I stirred when Roxy returned, but couldn't tell the time—the sky was navy blue out the roof panels.

Roxy yelled, "What the fuck?" and "Who are you?" and "Where's my *phen*?" and then Scott Lynn Miller's deep voice answering something I couldn't make out. I thought I heard Natalie, too, as the voices softened down to murmuring and blended into the surrounding noise, and I finally fell into a deep, empty sleep.

Scott Lynn Miller drove up on a mall security Segway, turned it gracefully, and backed up next to the bench where I sat with Katherine, a sales associate from the bridge designer department, and James, temporary manager of the Gap. Katherine and James chain smoked their way through the conversation, which ranged from the new district manager at our store, fresh out of a business school internship and doing things by the book, to James's having to institute timed breaks in his store since none of his employees, apparently, could tell the difference between 15 minutes and more-than-15 minutes.

Either Scott Lynn Miller was oblivious or innocent to the negative vibe that surrounded the three of us, because he leapt off the scooter and shook each one of our hands. "Scott Lynn Miller," he introduced himself, new to the job and the security game. I could tell by how Katherine lit his cigarette and James crossed the long, pointy toes of his dress shoes over one another that they, at least, found Scott Lynn Miller attractive. I didn't really think anything at all, which may be why he'd zoomed in on me.

"You aren't really smoking that," Scott Lynn Miller said.

I wasn't. I held a lit cigarette outside for 7 minutes once every two hours so that I could get a regular break.

"You've got the right idea," he said, as if I'd answered him. He dropped his own, only half-smoked, and crushed it under his foot with a decisive flourish. "It's a terrible habit."

After that, he'd always seem to be cruising by the bench on the Segway every time I popped outside to hold my ritual cigarette. We had short conversations, mostly impersonal, about the weather, the Wall Street protesters, and television shows. We had one talk when he told me about coming up to Seattle after Hurricane Katrina leveled his whole neighborhood, and taking a construction job with an uncle of a high school buddy until he cracked his head open on a piece of rebar and had to change careers. He was on a waiting list to either take the police academy test or enter the academy; I don't know which. And once, when I accidentally inhaled my cigarette while watching a sun-blind driver take down three no loading signs, he clapped my back until I stopped coughing.

I knew he knew my name because of my name tag. I was sure I hadn't told him my last name or where I lived, although it was possible I'd spoken of my parents or aunt and uncle, maybe Dei and Roxy, but in broad, round terms. But I was gypsy enough to not willingly tell a stranger anything truly identifiable about myself; not because I had anything to be ashamed of—or hide, except perhaps my origin, which, up until the previous night could have just been a fairy story, *xoxani paramicha*, and nothing else. But I was sure I didn't tell him my last name or address. I wasn't sure my co-workers knew either, even if he asked them.

I was alarmed. Maybe not as alarmed as I would have been, given a different context. It's understandable, considering, and, in retrospect *baXtali*.

Hot morning sun streamed through the open roof panel, and I sweated awake. Scabs set my hands into tender half-fists during the night, which cracked and leaked clear fluid when I opened them.

I stepped over Scott Lynn Miller, asleep on the kitchen floor, one of Tate's slippers pillowing his head. There was glass everywhere, so I tested each step before putting down my weight. The *ofisa* door was ajar; inside, Natalie and Roxy curled together across the sofa bed.

They both snored up the smell of stale beer. I poked Roxy gently to wake her, and she rolled over, threw her arm over her eyes, and made an unhappy sound. Then she sat bolt upright. "*Rovli*," she said. "What a fucking mess."

"I know," I answered. I pointed to Natalie, and Roxy shook her head, giving me the secret sister signals that we would talk outside, in private.

"What happened to your hands?" she asked, when we got outside.

"It's hard to explain," I said.

"You'd better try."

"I know," I said.

We made our way through the garden. Roxy bent over and grabbed her foot. Off balance, she nearly fell over into the dirt. "Glass," she yelled. "I got glass in my foot." She stepped down on her heel and hobbled to the hot tub. I followed her, and we pulled ourselves up onto the edge. I tried to pull the glass sliver from the ball of her foot, but my chewed-up hands wouldn't work right. She squeezed it out like a pimple and threw it over her shoulder.

"That *gadjo* said there was an earthquake." Roxy looked at me. "Really?"

No. "Yes," I said. "It was the strangest thing." I pushed down on my scabby palms, watching them turn white, then angry pink again. Clean fluid leaked out from under the scabs like water.

"That is the strangest thing." Roxy looked at me, hard. "I looked at the *ofisa* computer for news. There's nothing about even a small quake." She didn't break her stare. "The strangest thing." She blinked once, deliberate and slow. "That, well, and Scott Miller himself. Why didn't you tell me you were seeing a *gadjo*?"

I tried to meet her stare with one of my own, but I couldn't. "I'm not." I looked at my palms. The clear fluid gave way to thin blood. "I barely know him. He showed up after the…" I paused, telling on myself—a little subconsciously, a little on purpose— "—earthquake."

Roxy slid off the edge of the hot tub and spread her arms. "Oh, come on, Kiz." She leaned in. "There was no fucking earthquake." She leaned in closer. "Why'd you do it? To get Mamo and Tate home? To tell on me?"

I balled my bleeding hands, not believing what I was hearing. "You think I did this? You think it has something to do with you?" If my hands hadn't hurt so much, I would have punched her. "You think everything always has something to do with you, and if it doesn't, it can't possibly be important." I was so angry and didn't want to cry, but the more I tried to keep myself from crying, the faster the tears streamed down my face. "You are so fucking selfish."

She looked at me crying and sat back down on the edge of the tub. "Shit." and rubbed her foot. "I didn't mean that, *Rovli*. Not really. *Zhávo mánge*. I'm sorry."

It did the trick. "I know, Roxy," I said. I reached out and patted the back of her neck gently.

We sat still for a few minutes, both trying to ignore everything around us. Then Roxy asked, "So, what did happen last night?"

I didn't say anything, but she knew. She just needed something to remind her that she already knew. After all, we'd all been waiting for it.

"Oh, no," she said. "Oh, shit. Shit, shit, shit." Then she started to cry.

"It's OK," I said to her, not entirely sure it was. The words sounded hollow, but necessary.

"No," Roxy sniffed. "It isn't." She wiped her face and gave a strange smile. "You know what, *Rovli*? I am selfish. I don't want you to go." She grabbed my arm. "Partially because I don't want to lose you, but partially because I want to go. Natalie asked me to come home with her, and I told her yes." She leaned in and placed her cheek on my shoulder. "I don't want you to go. I want to go."

I placed my arm around her. "It's OK."

"No," she answered. "It isn't. I'm a terrible person. A terrible, selfish person."

"You aren't."

"Maybe." She pushed her face into the curve of my neck. "I don't really want to go," she whispered. "I just don't think I can stay."

We hugged one another, and the crying started again. We cried for each other and for ourselves. And in that crying, neither of us heard Scott Lynn Miller walk up and watch us. I don't know how long he stood there, because I had my forehead against Roxy's short, soft hair. He waited patiently, apparently, until both of us seemed cried out before finally interrupting. "I'll stay and help clean up," he said, as if that was what we were discussing. "Don't worry."

We sat up and looked at Scott Lynn Miller. Roxy rubbed the back of her hand against her face like an eraser and waited for me to answer. When I didn't, she said to him, "You don't have to do that."

"I want to," he answered. "I have some experience in this. Kizzy probably told you."

Roxy shot me a secret sister look, a what-the-fuck-is-he-talking-about look, but she was gracious and a quick liar. "Of course she did. We'd appreciate the help."

"I'd like to talk to Kizzy, if I could," he said.

Roxy bristled a little, weighing whether to leave me or not. I prayed she wouldn't. But she also didn't want to be there with him. "I'll make some coffee."

Scott Lynn Miller held out his hand to Roxy, to help her over a pile of glass by her feet. "That would be lovely."

Roxy gave me quick sister's glance, that she'd be right back, limped as gracefully as she could toward Mamo and Tate's *trela.*

Scott Lynn Miller hefted himself up on the side of the tub next to me. "I will help clean up," he said. "So don't be upset." He looked at me, at his feet, at me, then slid an arm around me.

"Scott Lynn Miller—" I started.

He dropped his arm. "I'd love for you to call me Scott."

"Scott Lynn Miller," I repeated. "What are you doing here?"

He turned to face me. "Let me explain."

Even with some distance between us, he was unbearably close. I felt like I didn't have a choice. "OK, then."

He looked back at his shoes, like what he wanted to say was written on them. "I have basically nothing to offer," he said. "After Katrina, well, even before Katrina, I didn't have anything. I mean, well, I do have *something.*" He glanced up from his shoes. "I have a child, Dan." He paused to let that sink in, then continued. "Anyway, my ex moved Dan up here, and after the storm, I followed."

"OK," I said. I wasn't sure what anything he said had to do with me.

"Anyway." He paused again, and shifted position. "Dan. I got Dan a goldfish like a month ago, and the goldfish just died, because, you know, goldfish just die. You've had a goldfish. You know what I mean."

I shook my head. "I never had a goldfish."

He smiled like I was joking. "Anyway," he continued. "So, Dan and I gave the fish a funeral. Dan is a little old for it, and did the whole eye-rolling, but I could tell it was important. We stood over the toilet, and I asked if Dan wanted to say a few words. And you know what the kid said?"

"What?" I looked at his hand, which was gripping the lip of the tub, awfully close to my leg.

"Dan said the fish, Joe, Dan named him Joe, had a full fish life and was happy when he died, having done and accomplished every fishy thing he wanted to. My child said this." Scott Lynn Miller seemed impressed.

I shifted my position, which he took as a signal to continue.

"There's something about you," he said. "I didn't have the guts to ask you out beforehand, and my kid, well, gave me the courage. I haven't done shit with my life yet, Kizzy. But, I want to die happy." He looked back again at his shoes. "So, I broke into Macy's personnel files to find your address."

I slipped off the edge of the tub hard onto my feet.

"It's probably a little creepy," he said. "But also, I hope, romantic." He looked around. "I tried to call you a bunch of times, but I never got ahold of you."

I broke into tears once more. Scott Lynn Miller spread a goofy, clueless smile on his face as he put his arm around me again. I wanted to shake it off, push him away, into the glass. I wanted to scream and scare him away, but I couldn't find the strength or courage. I wished him away as hard as I could, but the harder I wished, the harder he embraced me. I didn't return the embrace, but it didn't matter. He breathed in and out in my hair and held me close, only releasing me when Roxy emerged from the trailer with a tray of Turkish coffees. Scott Lynn Miller let me go and took a mug. I could feel the ghoul of his mouth, hot and damp, on my head. He slurped down some coffee and smiled again at Roxy.

She shook her head at him and tried to read my face as I took a mug for myself. I don't know what she saw, but she turned on and headed towards the *ofisa* with the remaining two mugs on the tray.

"Anyway," he said, "it's not much of a story, but there it is. What do you think?"

When I didn't answer right away but instead buried my face in the coffee mug to take a long drink, he took it as tacit agreement, and put his arm back around me. "So why do you only have the front of a house anyway?" he asked, at the same moment music blasted from the *ofisa* across the yard. It was Free Bird again. "If I stayed here with you, girl…" he sang, and squeezed his arm around me tighter, "…things won't ever be the same." He looked at me. "I love this song."

Growing up, Roxy and I helped out with both Mamo and Gracie's businesses; Mamo, because we were obligated as her progeny, Gracie because she hoped one of us would manifest a natural talent for a traditional, family trade.

Of the two of us, I was better at both cleaning and organizing for Mamo, and, to Gracie's slight dismay, the improvisational soliloquy needed to tell a good fortune. I was definitely better at understanding the fundamental theory behind the services my aunt and mother provided, which would be argumentatively lectured at us whenever the two women felt like Roxy and I should be somehow doing more or showing more interest in our futures.

"Everyone wants what?" Gracie quizzed.

"Money, sex, and power," was Roxy's answer. "To be loved, to belong, and to be unique," was mine.

"Everyone wants more than they deserve," Gracie would then say. "More than anyone deserves."

Mamo would tolerate this from Gracie for only so long before augmenting with her own mission, the fundamental way the two sisters, as well as their profession, diverged. "Everyone deserves. We just provide a little guidance on how to find it."

"Finding is easy," Gracie would shoot back, looking over her nose at Mamo. "Keeping is hard."

"Very true," Mamo would say. "But it's possible."

"Yes, possible. That's what we sell. What is possible," Gracie agreed. "People come to us to hear what is possible." She'd lower her voice then, to sound wise. "But it's rarely probable."

In the end, our mother and aunt would conclude on a single note, summed up by Gracie. "People are all the same," she'd say as Roxy and I were already half out the *ofisa* door, anxious to get back to whatever we'd been doing before being rounded up. Then, she'd add, louder, to make sure we heard, "But they're never who you think."

We debated the best way to clean up the broken glass. Scott Lynn Miller argued passionately for a rake, but the three of them got the farthest taking turns in the gardening gloves picking up the shards, piece by piece and depositing them into a bucket.

My hands rendered me nearly useless. But I walked around and picked up the biggest pieces, pain be damned, grateful to be doing something instead of sitting with Scott Lynn Miller's arm around my shoulder.

Natalie and Roxy took over the glass gathering process while Scott Lynn Miller and I righted Roxy and my trailer, which landed back onto the A-chassis with a great crash, shattering the last intact window. We filled the six buckets we had, and took a break, sitting together on the edge of the hot tub like a line of crows. We were debating where to dump the buckets when the *familia* came home. No one heard them until they were already there.

Gracie stood with her hands on her hips and a grimace that looked like we'd lost her a bet. Uncle Marko held up Dei, while Tate and Mamo stood behind them all, taking it in. The mess, the girls, the white boy, and me.

It was only a few seconds, enough for them to see Roxy grasping Natalie's hand and me lean away from Scott Lynn Miller.

There is no word in Romani for whatever I was, but the one for Roxy, Tate spit like poison. "*Pampuritsa*." The mess, the *gadjo* next to me, it didn't matter. Tate saw the girls' hands. "*Pampuritsa*," he repeated.

I lost my breath at the sound, but Roxy puffed up. She aimed back at him, but Mamo stepped into the line.

"Your *Káko* Fatlip called off the wedding," she said. "We tried to call and when no one answered, I worried."

I had my breath again. "It was my fault. Let me explain..." I paused, not really sure what I was going to say. But no one was looking at me anyway.

Mamo walked toward the hot tub with both Natalie and Scott Lynn Miller in her sights. "I think it's time for you to go," she said to them. "Both of you." She started to reach for them, when there was a terrible boom.

And the sky went dark, like the end of a scene.

The moment before, Roxy had been holding Natalie's hand. But now, in the dark, Natalie held Roxy's hand up over her head. Unnatural light pushed through her eyes like flashlights. They lit up her small face, perfect with a symmetry I hadn't noticed before.

Scott Lynn Miller's hand rested on my shoulder, heavy and dumb, like a bag of groceries. It was all I felt.

I saw the shadows of my family, Tate roaring again with hateful words, *Káko* Marko lowering Dei to her knees, and my Aunt Gracie with fists by her side. Mamo holding the edge of the hot tub. I saw my sister with her hand held by an alien. We all had our mouths open like hungry babies.

There are alternate versions of the Lallah Pombo story. Uncle Fatlip's second wife, Hope, an Austrian Sinti, told a version where Lallah Pombo finds the rain, but when she returns, it is too late and all she has left are the stories of her people and what she had seen.

Other versions of the story say that the rain, or a god, or creator, or a great sower in the sky gave Lallah Pombo a choice; she could save her people and be left alone, or die with them. In one telling, her presence itself is what sets the whole world out of balance, but there are a number of other versions in which it isn't, but she is hung out to dry to protect someone else who stole something or said something or kissed someone that actually instigated the crisis. In about a third of the stories, she sacrifices herself to save her people and becomes the rain, or the god, or creator sower, a star in the sky. In another third, her people sacrifice her to make things right; sometimes she fights to the end, sometimes she goes willingly.

The ship was above us, but we couldn't see it. Instead, that darkest dark pushed down like a low ceiling while the air rubbed on us with a heavy, woolen charge. The truck and Tate's van honked together, a chorus of metal ducks, and Free Bird flipped on and off from Roxy's laptop, over in the *ofisa*: *"…must be travelin' on now…"*

Mamo understood. "They came," she said. "I can't believe they came." She looked at me, alarm coming off her skin like a fever. "They came to take you."

"We did," Natalie said. Her voice was large, merged with the light from her eyes to become a thing, in and of itself. "But now we are taking Roxana."

"…places left to see…"

Roxy snatched her hand back from Natalie and cradled it like a burn. "What do you mean?" she asked. "Taking me?"

"I asked if you would come home with me."

"You trapped me," Roxy said. "You lied."

"I didn't lie," Natalie answered. "I came for her, but fell in love with you."

"…you, girl…"

"It wasn't planned or expected," Natalie continued. "But this project was designed with rigorous desire for experiential knowledge. That requires loose margins." Natalie reached again for Roxy's hand, but she wasn't quite ready to give it again.

"*...free as a bird now...*"

Our sounds broke through the charge and silence. Mamo wailed; Tate roared. Scott Lynn Miller clamped down on me with unexpected power and asked, terrified, "What is going on?"

I'd forgotten he was there. I slapped off his arm like it was a mosquito. The thing, Natalie's voice and light, hovered before me. It waited for me to say something, but I leaned around it and toward Natalie herself. The geometry of her face, the exaggerated pyramid of her fingers. I didn't see it but I hadn't been looking.

"We wouldn't take both," Natalie said to Mamo. "That is too cruel."

"I wasn't expecting this," Mamo said. "Not like this."

"No one was," Natalie said.

Our father came behind Mamo and held her shoulders. "You can't have her," he hissed, at Natalie, at the light.

Roxy took Natalie's hand again. "I'm not yours to give, Tate," she whispered.

"And this bird you cannot change..."

"Kizzy is as human now as anyone," Roxy said. She kissed Natalie's hand. "I'm the alien."

"*Lord knows, I can't change.*"

We see what we want to. We understand what we want to. We think everything applies to us, and it is only in retrospect that we see when it wasn't, when we weren't the star, the center, the protagonist of our own life. Sometimes, we are supporting roles. Still essential, still crucial, but as an element, a crucible, or a catalyst.

There is never a way to say goodbye. Roxy threw herself into my arms last. "*Rovli*," she whispered.

Then she stood next to Natalie and looked, one last time, at all of us.

I couldn't watch, so I looked at the ground. The unicorn lay exactly where I'd sat the night before. I swooped for it and threw it at my sister, just as the light thing curled around them.

The unicorn bounced off the tube of light, and I caught it and yelled for Roxy. A hand—my sister's, Natalie's—waved through the light like it was clearing away cobwebs, and I pushed the doll into the hand. It clasped the unicorn and pulled it in. Then they were gone.

We stood in the yard for a long time. We looked up until our necks ached, and then a little longer than that.

Scott Lynn Miller broke the silence. "I don't know what happened here tonight, and I want some answers." He grabbed my arm. "What are you?" Rage and confusion made him careless, and he twisted at me, clasping hard on my battered hands.

I yelped in pain.

"What are you?" He asked again and again, snatching at whatever he could of me. "What are you?"

I ducked him as best I could, but he kept coming. Tate stepped between us and picked up Scott Lynn Miller in his big hands and slammed him once against the side of the hot tub. If it'd been anyone else, the crack would have made me sick. Tate dropped him like a sack onto the dirt and broken flowers.

"What is she?" Scott Lynn Miller asked, his voice barely a whisper. He tried to find his bones and joints and push himself up.

Tate shoved him back down with his foot. "She's my little girl," he answered. "Now get the hell out of here."

I didn't watch him leave. I only know he did, muttering and confused. Tate stood between Mamo and I, his arms around us, as we all watched the sky again. Eventually, Gracie brought us out glasses of water.

I took the water from Gracie like I was coming out of a long dream. Gracie stood next to me while I drank, and after a while she took my hand. She turned it over carefully and pulled up the bandages to look at my palms. "Kizzy," she said. "When these cuts heal, there's going to be deep lines."

Part Two: Across the Universe

Sexing chickens is the easiest job to get in Sartorus, Mississippi. It is also the hardest to keep.

No one knows exactly how it is done. The factories give you two weeks at half wage, sit you with a chicken sexer to watch and figure it out. The attrition rate is tremendous; by age 16, nearly everyone you have ever known, has, at one time or another, trained as a chicken sexer, but you've only known one person who kept the job—Jonas' father—and he is the one that gets you the trial run.

They don't sit you next to Jonas, though. They sit you next to Cocoa, a south Louisiana Creole with a 95% accuracy rate. She finds you a stool, then drags over a steel cart stacked with trays. Each tray is packed with chicks so young they are still shiny with wet mucus and blood. Everyone seems to overlook the shrill cheeps and the mildew tang in the air.

Cocoa starts right away. "You pick dem up, den you—" she says, grabbing one with her left hand and squeezing it slightly over the plastic tub until she gets a quick jet of ashy water, "—clean out dey system."

When she looks at you, you are blinded by her headlamp.

"You wit me, boy?"

You nod.

Cocoa holds the chick close to your face. "Den you look hyeah—" she says, poking at the baby chick's ass, "—for da slit or da bump."

You see a bump. Later, you will learn the proper names for a chick's ass and slit or bump itself. You'll train new chicken sexers, and call the ass a cloaca, the slit a vent, and the bump the bead protuberance. But today, you nod again.

"Now tell me, boy or girl?" Cocoa asks, with a note of triumph in her voice.

"A boy," you answer. This isn't so hard.

"Nyah," Cocoa replies. The triumph turns into a giggle. "I fooled you. Das a girl." Cocoa tosses the chick into a large bin. "Dey all got a bump and a slit. Das not how you tell." She picks up another chick, milks out its shit, and holds the chick in her fist, stroking its head with a finger. She turns to you again, the light in your eyes. "I'll tell you de secret, boy. You gotta look at de shape datde bump and de slit make. Den listen to your voice. You got no voice, you got no job."

"Voice?" you ask.

"Inside your head," Cocoa says, like you have no sense. "It will just tell you if dey is a boy or a girl. Like, how long you need to think to see I'm a girl? You get de same thing with dem." She shoves the chick, bottom first, at you. "Dis one?"

You barely have time to look at the chick when Cocoa pulls it away. "Girl," you say.

Cocoa smiles at you. Her headlamp obscures everything but her teeth. "Good," she says, tossing the chick into the female bin and reaching for another off the tray. "Again."

At the motel, you ask the maid for extra blankets and pillows. "My son builds forts," you say. "It helps him deal with losing his mother." You have said this four or five times now to four or five maids, and each time it sounds more raw, more true.

The maids have sad, smiling eyes and bring you stacks of bedding you tack up over the windows and the ceiling with drywall pins. Wool and down are the best insulators, but acrylic is what you usually get.

Danny never helps prepare the room. He is just like his mother, who isn't dead like you've suggested to four or five maids but is, for all intents and purposes, lost to both of you now. Sometimes you look at Danny and wonder if, aside from hair color and blood type, there really is any of you in him. You look at him now, and he purposefully looks everywhere but back at you. He plays a game where he shifts weight from one foot to the other.

The blankets make the room dark. The air seems thicker, which lets you know the acrylic is scrambling your outgoing theta brain waves. Satisfied you're safe for the moment, your stomach growls. Danny leans right, then left. And even though it's closer to late lunch, you ask, "How about some breakfast, sport?"

The idea breaks his concentration. "Can we have McDonald's?" he asks.

"There isn't a McDonald's here at the motel," you answer. "We'll go to the coffee shop out front. You can have French toast."

"I bet there's a McDonald's somewhere," Danny grumbles.

There always is, you think, and, in truth, you could use a break from motel coffee shop breakfasts yourself, but the longer you are exposed, the riskier it is, the closer to being caught. You have to march Danny out the door and through the parking lot to the coffee shop. He's gone from shifting his weight to dragging his feet.

"I hate French toast!" he yells as soon as you are seated in a booth.

"Have something else," you say to him, as you look over the menu. You wonder why every motel coffee shop has "garden" in its name. "Have a hamburger."

"I hate hamburgers!" Danny yells.

The waitress has the same kind of sad, smiling eyes as the maids do, and she offers Danny special pancakes with a chocolate chip and banana face. The way she describes it, even Danny can't hate it. You order coffee and scrambled eggs because you know you can't waste an egg and you want to set an example.

"I'd like to make it to Kentucky day after tomorrow, the latest." There's a pair of researchers there offering an interview and a few days of both room and board, and any money you could save is good. Eggs and pancakes and motel rooms are killing you almost as much as gas.

Danny bobs his head as he chews. Then he pushes away his plate, still half full, and takes off his hat. He holds the hat in his hands under the table.

"Finish your breakfast, sport," you say. "And put your hat back on."

"I'm full," Danny whines in your ex-wife's voice. "And the hat is itchy and ugly."

Itchy you can see. The hat is made of boiled wool, thick and warm and greasy with protective lanolin. Ugly, you don't understand. It's a buffalo-plaid aviator style, with clips to hold up the earflaps if you want. You are wearing one just like it, in a different plaid. "I said finish your breakfast and put the hat back on." You push the plate back towards him.

He acquiesces and puts on the hat, but pushes the plate back. "No-o."

This catches the sad, smiling waitress' attention, and she holds up a pot of coffee in offering. You shake your head, more angry at the attention than anything. "Finish your breakfast, Chris."

Danny stabs at his pancakes with his fork. "Dad, I don't want to be Chris anymore."

"I told you to pick a name you can live with," you say, quietly. You hope he will notice and answer you quietly.

"I want to be Danny again."

You place your hand on the hand Danny is using to carve up the pancakes. This is partially to comfort him, partially, again, to get him to be still and quiet. "You can't, sport," you say. "We both have to be new people."

Danny shakes off your hand and pushes himself up from the table like a salesman at the end of a deal. "I didn't ask for that," he says, and walks out of the restaurant.

"Neither did I, sport." You pick up the remnants of Danny's pancakes, fold them in half and stuff them into your mouth.

You find Danny facedown across the bed in your motel room, headphone clamped over his ears. The MP3 player was a Christmas gift from your ex-wife's parents. Neither set of grandparents would ever have gotten you such a thing—the equivalent, anyway—when you were Danny's age. Then again, you were a very different boy than your child. At 10, you were in charge of cleaning the house and school; by 12, cleaning the house, school, and walking your drunk father home, and then, at 16, you were juggling cleaning the house, school, walking your drunk father home, and chicken sexing.

You sit on the bed and turn on the television. The volume is low, and you can hear music leaking from Danny's headphones. You know the tune, although it takes you a few seconds to recognize it. The Beatles seem like an odd choice for a 10-year-old, but he must have downloaded his mother's music collection. She liked this sort of stuff. You don't mind it; you even know the words, and you mumble-sing along as you flip through TV channels. *Nothing's gonna change my world.* The TV shows do their work. Danny can't resist. He peeks, then rolls over and watches with you, although he keeps his headphones on.

Danny falls asleep first. It's hard to be annoyed with him when he is asleep. You have never regretted taking him with you. You considered it your responsibility: not only as his father, but as the one who potentially put him in danger by mentioning him. Your voice was drowned out by your pride.

When you wake up, the sun has gone down, and both of you are safe, attesting to the success of the blanket tent in absorbing and fragmenting your brain waves.

In the world, you estimate you have a prediction success rate of 85%, plus or minus 3%, which, statistically, you know is excellent. After graduation, you went full-time for a while at the egg facility, with a 94% accuracy rate, sexing nearly 1000 chicks an hour. You moved up into the top sexer spot after Cocoa succumbed to aggressive pancreatic cancer. Sometimes you miss it there: a 95% success rate at anything is something to be proud of.

Still, your 85% hasn't failed you lately. You figure you blew your 15% failure all at once, failing to see that Kizzy was from outer space.

You open the windows and let the late summer breeze wake up Danny. The freshness of it is startling. He showers first, then you.

Danny is sitting on his packed duffle bag by the time you towel off. He even has his hat on, pulled low over his eyes. This makes you smile; you read in a parenting magazine once that routine was good for children, and you are happy to see that Danny has settled into your new life. He has his headphones back on, though, which means he hasn't forgiven you entirely.

But—and you don't need your voice to confirm the truth—there will be a McDonald's at a rest stop or off the highway or someplace easy to drive through. That's not too much exposure, you think.

Danny will like that. You drop the latest in your long line of pay-per-minute cell phones in the motel trash before you go.

Dr. Cal Iverson and his wife, Arleen McConnell-Iverson, PhD, leave their front door open for you and Danny. "Arleen hopes that an unlocked door will encourage an abduction," Dr. Cal, joked on the phone. "Like they'd come through the front door anyway."

You want to tell him that is exactly how they would come in, but this is a quick, light, check-in call. You figure you'll have plenty of time to tell Dr. Cal about how the aliens look just like extraordinary ordinary people. Like beautiful-but-attainable women.

"So don't you worry about what time you get in," Dr. Cal said. "You and the kid come make yourself at home, and we will see you in the morning."

You set your trip odometer to zero when you finally pull onto the two lane highway just past Bowling Green. The Iversons' home is right past mile marker 6, set back from the road by a thin gravel drive. It's a modest place in need of re-roofing, close enough to see neighbors but not hear them, no trees tall enough to obscure the view in any direction. You pull up behind Dr. Cal's gray pickup truck, as described, and find the front screen unlatched, the door unlocked, as promised.

Danny stands on the threshold, unsure of what to do and more timid of knocking into something than you would have been at 12. You'd be more patient, but you are holding your travel case and his duffle bag, so you knee him gently in the bottom to get him to move into the front foyer toward the single lamp the Iversons left on in their living room.

It looks like a friendly stranger's living room would look: spongy rug beneath your feet, wooden end table and coffee tables and bookshelves with their posed and dusty items, a sectional with worn spots and throw pillows. "Dad," Danny whispers. "What are we doing here?"

"I told you," you say, putting down the bags at the foot of the couch. "Dr. Iverson and McConnell-Iverson want to interview me about some things. Remember?"

"Yeah. But I still don't get it." Danny still hasn't moved; he holds his little music player and headphones in his hand, drooping like a dead sea creature.

The sectional is obviously where you and Danny will sleep. On a rocking chair a few feet away, two white bed pillows and some neatly folded afghans, crocheted in stiff, acrylic yarn, give off a strong, clean, detergent smell. You toss the pillows onto the sectional, and unfold one of the afghans. It feels warm, but the weave is loose, loopy. It will not be adequate protection. "They're scientists," you answer, looking around for other blankets. "Independent researchers. They are very well known."

Danny sits down, still clutching his wires. "What do they want to talk to you about?"

"Well," you say, trying to formulate an answer as you search for maybe a quilt, a rug, something, and try and remember whether you had, indeed, specifically requested that the Iversons leave out extra blankets for you. But you just let the conversation trail off.

"I want to go home," Danny whispers.

Your foot catches something dense and soft, and for an involuntary second you think it is a body before realizing it is just a pile of good-quality wool blankets fallen to the floor. You pick them up and identify them as Pendleton, even in the dark, the thick felt your ideal for theta-wave insulation. "Let's try and get some sleep, sport," you say to Danny.

You aren't sure how to position the pillows on the sectional. The couch and the love seat meet at a right angle, so it's either head-to-head, foot-to-foot, or head-to-foot. Danny's your child, so you go for head-to-head.

Once Danny is settled on the love seat, you cover him with the afghan. His hair is shaggy, you notice, curling on the pillow and catching flashes of strange light from the lamp. You ruffle it affectionately. "We need to get your hair cut," you say.

Danny digs his head into the pillow. "I want to let it grow, dad. Like it was."

His hair had curled down to the middle of his back when you'd first started; you told Danny you had to cut it so no one would recognize him. But that wasn't the reason, and you don't want to get into it now, so you tuck an edge of a Pendleton beneath Danny, then over him, like a tent. "It smells like a dog!" Danny yells in his French toast voice, and you expect more of a fight as you tuck yourself in.

But none comes. And soon you both sleep.

Dr. Cal and Arleen don't play at being quiet, at letting you sleep in or apologizing for waking you. They are both already a muffin or two into the family-sized variety box when you and Danny pad into the kitchen. Arleen pours Danny an apple juice and you a black coffee. Dr. Cal is ready to get started, over breakfast even, and when Arleen explains that she has a morning of horseback riding planned for her and Danny, Danny shoves a whole lemon poppy seed muffin in his mouth in excitement.

"I don't know if that's a great idea," you start to say to Arleen, but she misunderstands that you mean whether she can be responsible for Danny rather than the risk of being out in the open. Before Danny can even look crushed, Arleen says, "Cal and I raised a daughter ourselves. Don't you worry. Danny and I will be fine."

You raise your eyebrow at Danny. He'd told Arleen and Cal his real name. You don't have time to be angry, though, only anxious, and say anything more than, "Danny, wear your hat!" because just as Arleen finishes her sentence, she and Danny are out the door, Dr. Cal is looking at you, and you are looking at the remnants of a blueberry muffin you do not even remember eating.

Dr. Cal tents his fingers. "So," he says. "Where do you want to start?"

"Not sure," you say. "Maybe at the beginning." You look at Dr. Cal, pen in hand, a fresh, clean legal pad. "Right?"

Dr. Cal waits.

"I knew," you say. "I knew she was different. That there was something. The way she caught the eye. She was so tall. And smooth. I was drawn to her immediately." You look at him for a reaction. There is none. "But, I had no idea she was from outer space."

"Mmm," says Dr. Cal.

"The very first day, I gave her all the business. Usually it works. With her, it didn't." You look at Dr. Cal to see if he understands. He is tapping the pen on his teeth, but has not written down a word.

"I gave her all the business. Flattery, asked her questions, leaned in, everything. And it didn't work. She had no interest in me." You realize you are repeating yourself, but it is because Dr. Cal just sits and looks and taps the pen. "Do you know what I mean? But I had no idea she was an alien."

"I bet I do," Dr. Cal says. "You're a handsome guy. In fact," he says, and reaches for another muffin with his non-pen hand, "Arleen used a great word this morning when she first got a look at you. Toothsome, I believe." He puts down the pen and concentrates on the muffin with a smile. "Toothsome." Dr. Cal peels the paper from the muffin. "Continue, if you would."

You stand up. "You aren't writing anything down."

Dr. Cal sets down the muffin and looks at you. The look isn't too far from the look Kizzy first gave you when you met. "You haven't given me anything to write down yet. You met a girl. She did not want to immediately fuck your toothsome brains out. I think I can remember that."

The fact that he is giving you a look like Kizzy did once makes you quiet down some, give everything a second, and try and listen to your voice. *Is he one of them? Is this a trap? Does he mean us harm?* But nothing inside you says yes to these questions, not even like the quiet little yes you got around Kizzy, quiet enough to ignore.

"You weren't abducted. You had a near-abduction. Tell me something I can use," Dr. Cal says, chewing on his muffin. "Something specific. Or surprising. Or verifiable. Or, preferably, all three. But at least interesting."

"Like what?" you ask.

Dr. Cal shoves the last of the muffin into his mouth and pulls a manila folder from beneath his legal pad. He pulls out a headshot of a blowsy blonde, coral lipstick wicking into the dry wrinkles around her mouth. The whites of her eyes have a green tint that makes you uncomfortable. "This," Dr. Cal says, pushing the photo across the dining room table toward you, "is Cynthia. She estimates she has been taken aboard alien ships at least twenty times. She's met reptilians, grays, cat people, you name it." Dr. Cal lets that sink in. He pulls another photo from the folder and lays it over Cynthia like a professional casino dealer. "This one is Jeff." Jeff poses with his chin tucked down like a bull about to rage. "Jeff was taken from a strip club by a black man who sounded like a white man who said he needed to change out the microchips in Jeff's head." Dr. Call slaps down another photo, and another, then another. "Jeanie. Grays tried to impregnate her. Sandra, here, also, although she says it was like making love with God and hopes it happens again. And Bruce. He went to a moon of Saturn that exists in another plane when he was only seven years old."

You study the photo of ginger-haired Bruce. He looks up and away in the image at something out of frame. Dr. Cal waits for you to say something. "What are grays?" you ask.

"Grays are what contactees and researchers, such as myself, call the humanoid aliens one thinks of when one thinks of aliens, UFOs, and associated phenomenon." Dr. Cal taps his pen against his opposite wrist. "Gray skin, large head, black eyes, short and squat…" He trails off, as if the rest were obvious.

"That's not what they look like," you tell him. You think briefly of Kizzy's auburn hair, her symmetrical and optimally proportioned features, her long spine slightly pushing up beneath her shirts. She was tall and, yes, slightly-alien looking. Then again, it was your experience that the prettiest women always looked a little alien.

Dr. Cal waits for you to say something, and when you don't, pushes himself away from the table, much like Danny at the diner the other morning. "OK," he says and points at the sectional, the pile of blankets. "Tell me about the hats. It's too warm for wool. And tell me about all this. This configuration here. You asked for extra blankets. You carefully and deliberately arranged them. Why?"

"Theta waves," you answer.

"Theta waves?"

"Brain…" you start, but Dr. Cal interrupts you.

"I know what theta waves are." He holds up his hand for you to wait, and gets his pen and pad. He comes back in and sketches the placement of the pillows and blankets.

You are relieved that you could give him something of interest. Dr. Cal is your ticket, and you know it. If the world is going to hear and believe that aliens are among us, it will have to come from someone credible. A doctor. A scientist. You are neither of these things. You are, as Danny's mother liked to remind you, nothing but a hick from Mississippi. When you were married, she said that playfully. When you divorced, she wielded it as the reason she fell out of love with you, the reason you always seemed to be losing everything and having to start over again, and the reason you shouldn't have more than monthly visitations with Danny.

Dr. Cal sucks his lip loudly as he draws. You are glad you decided to lay head-to-head with Danny, that your love and devotion will somehow be documented by Dr. Cal even if no one actively notices it. It would hold up in court, you think: *Your honor, I did what I thought was best for my child because I truly loved him. See?*

"So," Dr. Cal says. "The blankets block your brain waves? From getting out? Or theirs, from getting in?"

"Both."

"Where did you get the idea that this would work?"

"I don't know," you say. "It was just a gut feeling." Your answer embarrasses you. You know it was pieced together from what you could remember from movies and television, combined with what you remembered from high school biology and earth science. But it isn't like you crowned yourself and Danny with tin foil hats.

Dr. Cal double-checks to make sure he has an accurate representation of the sectional. You briefly consider suggesting he take a picture, but he is the doctor. He shakes his head to himself and then sits down heavily on the sofa. You follow suit, and sit down on the loveseat. When you do, you hear murmuring from beneath the blanket.

It's muffled, but definitely speech. Someone is beneath the blanket.

Someone is in the house.

Dr. Cal jumps up from the couch; you slide off. You are sick with panic and fear. This would never hold up in a court of law: *Your honor, I knew Danny shouldn't be out in the open, that they would come for us, I knew it,* but knowing didn't protect Danny, or Arleen or Dr. Cal, who pulls back a blanket with the end of his pen.

The voice gets louder, more musical. Dr. Can drops the pen and pulls back another blanket. You can see Danny, wrapped in light, Arleen, wrapped in light, like Kizzy's sister the night you saw her taken, when you stood in the broken-down yard with Kizzy and her extended family and you had no business being there. But you were. You ignored all good sense, all local laws. You were blind with wanting to see her, wanting to make her yours. You should have known when you first arrived at her house, trailers, blown over like a goddam natural catastrophe, that you should have turned right around and left. When you met her sister, shorter and squatter—now there was a gray, if you'd ever seen one—giving you the evil stink eye. But you didn't. You stayed. You slept like a dog on the trailer floor, you picked up broken glass with your bare hands like a fool. You ignored your voice.

You are lost in a million whirling thoughts when Dr. Cal grabs your face and shakes it between his thumb and forefinger. "Hey," he says, and spits a cold, wet poppy seed on you. "Are you all right?"

You aren't all right. You've failed. But then you see Dr. Cal holding Danny's MP3 player, a gift from your ex's parents, and then you hear it—*Jai Guru Deva*—tinny and distant through the white ear buds.

"We sat on this Walkman," Dr. Cal says. "It's OK. It was just music."

You splash water on your face and look in the mirror for a long time. You breathe in and out to try and slow your heartbeat, and you have a sharp cramp in your neck from clenching your jaws in fear.

Your face looks strange to you, like it is not what you expected to be looking out at, like you expected to see someone else in your reflection.

In truth, you did. Someone younger, someone calmer, someone who doesn't know what you know. The young man with the smile that your dad called "cocksure" and your friend Jonas once likened to a crow's. You liked the latter, and even tried for a while, without success, to adopt "Crow" as a nickname, but no one else would take up that banner.

Especially not Danny's mother. You met her at the factory. She had no talent for sexing chickens, and wept when you told her what happened to the baby boy chickens. That was the moment; you told her how they were chopped up by steel macerating machines, and as tears filled her eyes, you swept in like a cocksure crow and took her hand.

It was her idea to move to New Orleans after the wedding. There were more jobs there than at the factories, which she couldn't keep, and at the Dairy Queen, which she could keep but hated, or the IGA her parents owned or the American Legion Hall where your daddy drank.

She was right, of course. You got into construction, where you made good money, factory-good money. And she lied a little to get the job in the development department of the New Orleans Museum of Art, but it worked out well. She was good at asking for money. You got a row house in the Ninth Ward, and not too long afterward, she was pregnant with Dan.

You push your fingertips gently onto your eyelids. Pink and green lights, stars flash there and calm you. You remember when you were really little, way younger than Danny, asking your momma what those lights were, and she told you it was a peek at the light shows in heaven.

Even then, you suspected that wasn't true, but you always liked the idea.

Outside the door, you hear a commotion. Voices and doors and clanging in the kitchen. You rinse your hands again and go out to join Danny and Arleen and Dr. Cal.

Danny runs to you, something he hasn't done in ages. "Daddy!" he yells breathlessly, and buries his face in your chest and throws his arms around your waist.

When he lets go, he has caught his breath enough to let out the most words you'd heard from your child all trip long. "Daddy, oh my god! I rode a horse called a pinto, and she was chestnut and white and had a pink nose, like a bunny. Her name was Bean and I loved her and then Arleen and I sat and ate some graham crackers and peanut butter and green apples but I am hungry again. And I fed Bean some apples and she ate them right out of my hand. She has big teeth. Can I have a horse?"

And you find yourself nodding. Why can't Danny have a horse? There was no place to keep a horse right now and no money to pay for one either, but that didn't mean there wouldn't be.

Danny gapes, flabbergasted. You are nodding, and then you nod harder with the pleasure of it all. And Danny throws himself in for another hug. This one lasts a few seconds, and you look down and smell Danny's sweaty wool hat and remember how he smelled when he was a baby, and then a toddler.

"Wait until I tell mom!" Danny yells into your chest.

You stiffen, and this ends the embrace. Danny steps away, smiling like the day he unwrapped that stupid MP3 player from his mother's parents.

Arleen steps into view. "You said you were hungry?" she asked Danny, then answers his nod, "Let's go help Dr. Iverson make us all some sandwiches."

You follow them into the kitchen. Dr. Cal lets Danny slice tomatoes, with a sharp knife, and you wince, partially at the knife and still partially at the mention of telling his mother anything.

Arleen swipes a tomato from the cutting board and pops it into her mouth. Then she grabs another and offers it to you. You shake your head.

"So," Arleen says. "Danny said your ex—?" and pauses to ensure that, indeed, his mother is your ex-wife. At this, you nod.

"Danny tells me your ex-wife is travelling too?"

"Yes," you say, but Danny interrupts.

"She's traveling through Africa," Danny says. He forgets he is holding a sharp knife and brandishes it. "In like, deep, deep Africa. Like, villages and the savannah and jungles."

You think of how much easier it is to tell people, like motel maids, that she is dead. "There aren't jungles in Africa, sport," you say. "And be careful with that knife."

Danny looks puzzled for a second, then brushes it off in lieu of his excitement. "That's why she can't call me. There's no cell phones in Africa."

Dr. Cal looks up from arranging salami on a plate and exchanges a look with Arleen. Then he says, "Must be very remote."

"Like *Heart of Darkness* remote," Arleen adds.

"Very," you say. "Very remote." You hope that is the end of that, but Dr. Cal asks Danny what his mother is doing in Africa and moves the board of sliced tomatoes onto the table.

"She works for a museum," he says. "She's collecting stuff?" He looks at you for confirmation.

"Exactly right," you say.

"You must be very proud of her," Arleen says, and pats Danny on the shoulder. "Great job with the tomatoes."

The four of you make sandwiches. The tomatoes are evenly sliced, impressively paper thin. Damn if he didn't do a fine job with them, even being careless with the knife. You all eat in relative silence, although Danny radiates excitement like hot pavement gives off summer heat. You wish you could enjoy it, luxuriate in the joy of having a happy child, a child you made happy, but you are involuntarily filled with dread. Your voice is telling you something, only everyone's chewing is drowning it out.

After lunch, Danny volunteers for a nap. You can't believe how on you are with him, today. It makes you half want to call up Danny's mother. *Yes, Danny will need riding lessons. You can talk to him about it later. Right now, he's taking a nap.* You follow Danny into the living room, as Dr. Cal and Arleen rinse dishes. He grabs his MP3 player from the floor and snaps on his headphones and before you can cover him, he asks. "I can really have a horse?"

"Sure, sport," you say.

He smiles and presses play, and you pull and tuck the blanket over your child's head to the end of that damn song.... *Gonna change,* his headphones sing.

"Africa?" Dr. Cal asks.

It catches you by surprise, just as, you suspect, Dr. Cal hoped it would. "Yes," you say. "Dream of hers."

Dr. Cal writes something on the legal pad. He is taking more and more notes as you talk, but it doesn't make you feel good. In fact, it just heightens your sense of trepidation. "I'm just surprised," he says.

"Why?" You know the source of your anxiety—Danny, outside, for two hours, riding around. You sitting here in the Iversons' home, with its bay windows. Too exposed. You knew it as Arleen had ushered Danny out the door before you could protest, and the panic attack over the MP3 player sealed it.

"Just seems like an ex-wife and a mother would be a little more concerned about your and Danny's health and welfare than traipsing around Africa. I mean, you claim to have witnessed alien abduction. The presence of alien life on earth." Dr. Cal lays the pen down on the pad. "Even if she didn't believe you. Hell. Especially if she didn't believe you. Seems weird she'd leave Danny with you when you are obviously in a state."

"I didn't tell her," you say. So much easier to make her dead. "Seemed silly to worry her." Unlike when you say she is dead, the words sound untrue.

"I wouldn'tve left our daughter with Arleen if she was making claims like you are."

You understand this line of questioning. He doesn't care about the location of Danny's mother at all. "You don't believe me."

"I do, I do." Dr. Cal picks up the pen again. "Tell me more about the ship."

You are happy to get off the topic of Danny's mother. "I didn't really see the ship. But I knew it was there. I felt it, like a great weight pressing down on us, like it was about to press us flat." You hold your hands together as if about to pray, then open and shut them like a book. "Like pressed flowers."

Dr. Cal makes some notes. You wait until he is done.

"And there was noise. Not from the ship, that was silent. Not quiet, silent, like the absence of sound was noticeable. But there was honking, alarms from cars, revving on and off with the radios turned up real loud."

"Talk about the light again," Dr. Cal says.

"It was solid," you say. "A luminous cylinder. A conduit. It led up to the ship. Kizzy's sister and the other alien, they stepped into it, and it took them up."

"Did you feel anything? Smell anything?"

"It happened so fast. Then, like I said, Kizzy's father attacked me. I barely got out of there with my life."

Dr. Cal sat and read over his notes. When he looked up, he considered what he was going to say. "Will you go on record with all this?" He slid down his glasses and peered at you over the top to emphasize this was an important decision.

"Of course."

"Now, going public with this—it will change your life. Remember those people I showed you? Bruce and Jeff? And Cynthia?"

You think of Cynthia's green eyes and shudder a little. "Yes."

"Nothing was the same for them once they committed to their stories. Jeanie lost her job and then her house. Jeff, well, his family petitioned the court system to have him involuntarily committed. Sandra's marriage broke up. Bruce had to move from his hometown and change his name, the harassment got so bad. There are real consequences to this. What I said about your ex-wife? Well, that might come into play now. She could try and take Danny from you. A judge might let her." Dr. Cal scoots his glasses up and down his nose. "And I think you know all these potential dangers because you came in giving us a fake name."

Your mouth drops open a bit. You could really throttle that kid.

"It's OK, it's OK," Dr. Cal waves it away. "I'm not insulted. We're in a funny business, Arleen and I. It's just, I think you obviously have a basic understanding of what you are in for, with the fake name. But just, maybe, not the whole of it."

"You don't think I should go public?"

Dr. Cal slides his glasses off and pinches the bridge of his nose. "I don't think you have enough to warrant the effects this will have on your family. On your wife..."

"Ex-wife," you correct.

"Ex-wife. And Danny. Danny's getting to the age where what people say matters a lot."

"I can protect my child."

Dr. Cal points the earpieces of his glasses at you. "See? That's what I mean. You see Danny as a child. Just like any father. But Danny is a budding young—"

You hold up your hand. "I see just fine."

Dr. Cal sighed deeply. "If you want to press on, I will refer you to a colleague up at the Center for UFO Studies. In Chicago. Fine man. A physician. His partner is a psychiatrist. They will videotape your statement, and give you a battery of tests – brain scans, personality assessments, sleep lab, hypnosis, the whole caboodle." Dr. Cal puts his glasses back on. "When does your wife… ex-wife return from Africa? The tests are grueling and can take weeks. Danny should be at home. It'll be hard on you, hard on the kid."

"Danny stays with me."

"It'd have to be under your real name," Dr. Cal adds.

"Fine," you say, thinking that it's actually not fine at all, but willing to cross that bridge when you get to it.

Arleen sniffs loudly to signal that she has entered the room. In the sun, frizzled silver hairs catch the light, giving her a corona. Dr. Cal looks helplessly at his wife, and she joins you at the table. "Calvin's right, Scott. Danny could use a break."

"Danny stays with me."

Arleen shakes her head. "You haven't even told Danny anything. The kid thinks you are on the 'worst family vacation ev-er.'" Arleen does a fair job of capturing Danny's whine. Then she shakes her head again, but with a smile. "God, Danny's a sweetheart. Reminds me of our Heidi at that age. Our daughter."

"Danny stays with me."

"Well," Arleen says. "I think you should at least tell Danny."

On cue, Danny pads into the kitchen, rubbing one eye. "Tell me what?"

You sit Danny down, and at the Iversons' kitchen table, you tell him everything. About meeting Kizzy at work, courting her, going to her house, and then about how an alien ship came and took away her sister and a houseguest, just like that.

"Cool," Danny says.

He gives you a look you can't define at first. You soon realize it is a look of respect.

"So, was she like the movies? All slimy and evil? Like in *Alien*? Or *District 9*?"

"No. She looked like you or me."

"Does Mom know?"

"No."

"Can I tell her? About the horse and the alien?"

"Sure, sport. Sure." You place your hand over Danny's hand so he knows what you are about to say next is very important. "The Iversons think I should take you home, but I'd like to take you with me to the UFO Institute. What do you think?"

"No way!" Danny yells in his French toast yell. "I want to go to the alien place."

"Then, it's settled," Dr. Cal says.

You let Danny talk you out of your hat, then comb and fuss over your hair. Using the same bathroom mirror you stared into earlier, you fix up your sloppy shaving job. You borrow an iron from Arleen, and touch up the one dress shirt you have with you.

You want to look nice in the photograph Dr. Cal takes for his archives.

Or at least sane. Reasonable. Rational.

And even though you feel quite victorious, when the moment comes, when Dr. Cal says, "Smile," you can't do more than wince a little in response.

Outside Louisville, you pull into a gas station and fill up, buy a new, cheap cell phone, and a bag of gummy worms for Danny. You figure it'll take you about seven hours to the Illinois border, which gives you plenty of time to drive leisurely, maybe stop someplace and let Danny have a little fun. Then you can find a motel room in Gary, Indiana for the night, hit Chicago first thing in the morning.

Danny sits in the passenger seat with his legs crossed and tucked beneath him, like a yogi. You marvel at the contortions your child can twist into. You think you should encourage him to try out for wrestling. In fact, you do. You say, "Do they have a wrestling team in middle school?"

Danny doesn't hear you over the music blaring in his ears. At this rate, you think, he'll be flexible but deaf as a doorstop by puberty. You pinch his knees, and he pulls out one ear bud.

"Do they have a wrestling team up at the middle school?"

"I don't know," Danny says, suspiciously. "Why?"

"You should go out for it, bendy like you are."

Danny violently bites the head off a gummy worm. "Are you serious?" He chews, plugging the bud back into his ear. "No way, dad."

You turn on the heater, even though it is warm enough in the car. You are between radio signals, and without the hum of the air, you can just hear snippets of Danny's music.

"I have to go to the bathroom."

"Want me to just pull over?"

Danny shoots you a withering look. He wants a real toilet. There's a sign for a rest stop 13 miles ahead, and you drive the rest of way without saying anything else.

The car seems to glide in total silence. Up ahead, it is so flat, you can see a thunderstorm in front of you, the rain falling like a dark curtain. You speed up, as if you want to catch it, or at least make some noise.

You never noticed that, indeed, like the saying, it is often quiet before a storm, until Katrina. Not that you noticed the quiet before she landed, but, after living through her, you pay close attention to all storms.

You break your own silence. "You ever think about the hurricane?" you ask Danny.

Danny solemnly removes his ear buds to answer the question. "Yes," he says.

You are tempted to ask Danny what he remembers, but now he stares out the window at the thunderstorm with alarm, and you feel guilty bringing it up. Whatever he remembers, you remember too. You carried him in your arms as the waters rose, even though he was already too big to be carried and his dangling feet kicked your shins with every step. Your ex-wife hurried to keep up. You carried Danny all the way to Canal Street, his face buried in your neck against the floating bodies and the fires. At the casinos, police directed the crowd towards the Dome. Your ex-wife didn't want to go there. Not with the rest of the angry, hungry crowd. She pointed at some teenagers holding baseball bats. When you asked where she wanted to go, she said, "Gretna." In Gretna, her boss had a big, fancy house and probably enough supplies for three more. We'll go there, she decided, but once she'd decided, it was up to you to make it happen. You carried Danny and led your ex-wife across the Crescent City

Connection, only to face a wall of shotguns blocking the way into Jefferson Parish. "Turn back!" riot gear barked through megaphones, and with your tired arms and shaking child and angry ex-wife, you turned around and didn't stop again until you were inside the Superdome.

Eventually, your ex-wife got a line through to her boss. He paid off police and militia and drove to the Dome in a big, long car. Your ex-wife climbed into the front seat, and you opened the back door, placed Danny inside, and even buckled the seatbelt. But you couldn't bring yourself to get in.

You watched the big, long car glide away the same way it came. Your ex-wife turned her head, and you each watched one another—her leaving, you staying—long after it seemed physically possible.

The rest stop is cold and quiet and green-smelling, even with the green obscured by light, white frost. As Danny uses the facilities, you look at the glass enclosed bulletin board advertising the amenities of the area. Apple picking—it's the wrong season. Pumpkin patches, also wrong season. Winery tours, no. Doll museum, no. Batting cages and go-karts. You point out this last one to Danny after he emerges, wiping his hands on the sides of his pants.

"I don't want to go to batting cages," he says.

"Would you rather go to the doll museum?" you ask, sarcastically.

"I'm not a baby."

"Well, what do you want to do? I feel like we should do something you want." You want to apologize for bringing up the hurricane, and Danny seems to understand.

Danny pulls out his ear buds and looks at you, almost like you'd promised a second horse. "Can we go to the outlet mall?"

You didn't even notice the ad for the outlet mall, twenty-five miles ahead.

"I could use some new clothes." He brushes down at his pants where he just wiped his hands. "These are gross."

"Really?" you ask, and Danny smiles, nodding enthusiastically.

Sometimes you look at Danny and wonder if, aside from hair color and blood type, there really is any of you in him. But then you see how he bobs in his seat, gummy worm floppy between his teeth as he chants, "Outlet mall! Outlet mall!" and realize he is like you, easy to please.

So be it, you think, put the car in drive and pull onto the highway.

The Center for UFO Studies is nothing more than a storefront between a nail salon and a boarded-up travel agency, stuffed with shabby, mismatched office chairs and lined with laminate bookshelves. You aren't sure what you expected, but it was more impressive than this, although the receptionist looks appropriately friendly and bored, and Dr. Davidson has a solid handshake.

Even the sad airport motel you are staying in has better quality furnishings.

The first few days, you took Danny in with you. He sat in the reception area and the receptionist brought him apple juice and Lorna Doone cookies from the gas station on the corner, and even let him use her computer to surf the Internet and recharge his MP3 player. The receptionist was nice and didn't complain, but you figured she didn't get paid nearly enough money to also be a nanny.

Today, you left Danny with enough money to get a sandwich and some magazines from the motel gift shop, even though you really can't spare any more, and, in fact, money is beginning to really worry you. Dr. Davidson thinks there is nothing unethical about selling your story when you are a contactee, especially since so many contactees wind up losing their jobs.

You aren't so sure it is a great idea. You wonder if you can find someone that can make you an honest-to-god fake identification with your new name on it. Danny can stay Danny, but at some point, you are going to have to put down roots, send him back to school, find some income, and you don't think anyone after you is going to be giving up the chase anytime soon. You know that as well as you know the sun is hot, water is wet, and what a baby girl chicken looks like right out of the egg.

The next morning, you arrive early for your appointments, with Danny in tow. You need to ask the receptionist for two favors, and you want to be able to return Danny to the motel if she refuses the first.

Her name is Olga. She is a graduate student at the University of Chicago, working on her doctorate. She's a pretty girl, made prettier with her long cascading mane of shiny black hair. Danny immediately told her, upon first meeting, that it looked like the tail of a horse. You were grateful Olga took that as a compliment and even more grateful that she didn't seem to mind Danny's presence while you were in the back offices.

Olga looks up at you like she was expecting you, which, of course, she was. She starts to check you in, but you stop her.

"Olga, I have to ask you for two huge favors. First, could Danny stick around here with you today?"

"Of course," she answers. "Danny is a lot of fun."

"Secondly," you start, and if having your hat off didn't make you so nervous, even here, you would have wrung it between your hands. "You know I have a sleep lab tomorrow and…"

"And Danny has no place to stay," she finished. She brushed back a few strands of her amazing hair that had wandered into her face. "I'd be happy to watch him. I live with my mother on the south side, and I know she'd be just thrilled."

"I'd be happy to compensate you."

"No, no. You have not met my mother. She would really love it. She says I'm too old to be any fun." Olga shakes her head, letting loose a few other strands. "Besides, tomorrow is that transmission party. I know Danny would want to do that beforehand." She leans up a little from her seat behind the desk. "Right, Danny?"

When it comes to you, Danny can never hear anything over his music. But you notice that as soon as Olga throws a few syllables toward him, he is up and at them, at the desk, having heard everything.

"Yes!" Danny yells. "I almost forgot."

Olga explains that to celebrate NASA's 50th anniversary, as well as the anniversary of the launch of Explorer I, the United States' first satellite, and the 45th anniversary of the Deep Space Network, a system of radio antennae sweeping the sky for extraterrestrial communications, NASA was planning on transmitting a digital version of a song into deep space at exactly 6 PM Central time.

"Guess what song, Dad. Guess what song," Danny interrupted.

When you don't answer immediately, Danny and Olga burst out, simultaneously, "Across the Universe."

"You know, Dad. That Beatles song. You know it. You sang along with it in the motel that time," Danny says.

"So, the Center is having a little party at the University. We'll bundle up really good and head to the roof of the Astrophysics and Space Research lab and blast the song at the same moment. There will be people all over the world playing the song at the same time." Olga smiled. "Then we come inside, and there will be hot chocolate and hot cider, and a little buttered rum for the adults. I'm sure Dr. Davidson mentioned something."

You aren't sure. Really, the tests have all been a bit of a blur. You probably would have remembered something, though, since it was that damn song. Since the scare with Dr. Cal, you have decided you hate everything the Beatles ever performed.

But Danny is looking at you with his horse and outlet mall look, and you won't say no. Besides, it's a favor to Olga, who obviously is excited about the party, and she is going above and beyond. Seems only fair you should too.

It's a windy, clear Monday evening when you arrive at the University with Danny. Danny is excited about the party, excited to spend the night with Olga and her mother (he keeps telling you, "She's 23!" like it is an accomplishment) and, either in deference to the cold or in a show of gratitude, Danny has voluntarily donned the boiled wool hat. In fact, Danny remarks that it is cool the two of you match when you wear the hats, a comment that fills you with pride even as you suspect you have Olga's enthusiastic influence to thank.

You feel a foreboding. Your voice is telling you to beware, but of what, you don't know. Olga is completely trustworthy, and her mother, Mrs. Cervenko, a kindly babushka-type, according to every doctor and PhD associated with the center.

You suppose it has something to do with the tests tonight. You will be in a sleep lab, wired up and watched, as you attempt to fall into a normal sleep in a hospital-looking bed. You doubt your ability to sleep on command, sleep while being watched, and to sleep in a bed that reminds you of sickness and death.

Dr. Davidson assured you that the tests were necessary and, in fact, were a key part of his current main studies. He explained that he did not believe that alien abductions were a side effect of a specific type of sleep apnea, which caused hallucinations as a patient transitioned into or out of sleep. Even though you were wide awake during your experience, Dr. Davidson explained, gathering more data on sleeping contactees could only help disprove the hypothesis.

You understood. Data meant money. You understand needing money. Just like it is not wrong for contactees to sell their stories, it isn't wrong for the scientists to milk research grants for every dime they're worth.

Dr. Davidson spots you first. He ruffles Danny's hat like it is his hair and gives you one of his good handshakes. "Go on in," he says. "We'll check you into the lab at 7, Scott, and I'll drive you there, so you have some time to relax and enjoy."

There are a bunch of scientists and UFO-enthusiasts milling around, and you are loathe to join them. Danny, however, spots Olga sitting with what you figure to be, based on their age and rumpled appearance, her fellow graduate students, and makes a beeline to them.

You wonder what it is that has made Danny so comfortable around older kids. Not even kids. Young adults.

You straighten your hat and move toward the card table stacked with refreshments.

Something in your hand is better than nothing in your hand.

You have a hot chocolate, then a hot cider, and have to urinate just as the group starts to mobilize for the roof, University AV boom boxes in hand.

You follow the restroom signs, but not before you hear Danny over the crowd yell at you, "You aren't going to miss this, Dad, are you?" and you shake your head widely so he can see.

You are, indeed, going to miss it, but you know the assurance is enough; once they are on the roof, Danny won't even notice whether you are there or not. You see him holding Olga's hand as they rush along with the crowd toward the stairwell.

You follow the signs to the restrooms, your bladder getting more and more insistent as you realize the signs have taken you in a complete circuit of the building and back to where you started. Only, you aren't alone.

When your ex-wife was driven away in her boss's long car, when she looked over her shoulder and you held each other's gaze for an impossibly long time, was the last time you ever looked your wife in the eye.

The first year was easy. She was in Seattle; you were still in New Orleans. Once the flood waters receded, there was plenty of construction work, even though much of it was unpaid. Your FEMA check covered your expenses very well, and your ex-wife never asked for any support, which was more about the fact that she didn't want anything from you, you knew, than that she didn't need anything.

Then, you got beamed in the head by something—stories varied, depended on the witness, none of whom could be squarely counted on. Like you, the men who stayed behind to help clean up were not always the most reliable men in the world. You recovered from the head injury in a hospital in Bogalusa on the government's dime, but you wouldn't be going back to construction, the doc said, in no uncertain terms. After a second, third, even a fourth opinion at a temporary community clinic, you realized you weren't going to make a living there any longer, that you were missing your kid growing up, and so, you took the last of your FEMA money and followed your family to the Pacific Northwest.

When you'd pick up Danny for your visits, you still never looked your ex-wife in the eye. You looked at her chin, her ear, at a spot on the floor right in front of her feet or directly behind her.

Until today. Until right now. You couldn't miss her, standing by the card table, tapping her foot like she was expecting you and you were late.

So you greet her. "Hello, Danielle."

"Hello, Scott," she says. In those two words, you hear more than a greeting. You hear: I was worried, why'd you do it? I will end you, and it is going to be OK. You move closer because you are sure there is more you can read from her, and you need to see her face more clearly.

When you get close, she punches you in the face.

You reel backward, taking over a chair with a fold-out desk, and land on your ass. You almost piss in your pants.

You forgot she had quite a left.

Then she stands over you, helping you up. Her face changes into relief and pain, and she cries. She still loves you. She cries like she did the first time you met her, back in the factory. This time, however, you, not the injustice of what happens to unwanted baby boy chickens, are the cause of her suffering. So, you hold her to you, and she whispers in your ear, "Kidnapping in the first degree will get you at least two years under Washington State law." She squeezes you in her arms. "Thank god your friends the Iversons tracked me down." She then pushes you away. "I'm going to try and get you the maximum sentence, you son of a bitch."

"I know," you say, as if you agree. You don't, but not because you don't think a court would convict you. You really want to get to the roof. You're filled with that uneasy feeling, the anxiety; your voice is yelling clearly now. The broadcast above is meant to be heard, and it will be. As hard as Danielle has been looking for you, the aliens have been looking harder. They are getting closer. Soon, they will be here.

And you will be gone. You are certain of it. As certain as you are that you no longer have to piss as badly as a few seconds before, as Danielle's punch is going to leave a shiner, as the sun rises in the east and sets in the west: the aliens are going to take you away.

Over your ex-wife's head is a moon-faced clock. This clock is the same kind of clock found in every school, every institution, and a number of workplaces. You have watched clocks like this many times in your life, waiting as the arms sweep around to whatever the desired hour and minute would be in that situation, whether the end of last period in high school or the end of a shift at work.

In this one, you watch as the hour and minute hit 6 PM. Above you and your ex-wife, a wall of sound, all at once, building to crescendo and then lulling, building. If it is this loud going down through closed windows and the cinderblock and concrete construction, it must be a solid column reaching upward:

Words... flowing... like endless rain in... a paper cup...

Your ex-wife is shaking you by the shoulders. There are so many things you want to tell her. After you met her, you let more than a few boys slip through your station, to give them a chance at life. They said you were slipping, but you weren't wrong. You knew it. You did it for her.

...slip away across the universe...

You look at her, and she is glowing. It's anger, but it reminds you of when she was pregnant with Danny. You were on the porch of your row house, and there was a warm rain. She was huge. She placed your hand on her belly and asked, "Boy or girl?"

She only asked you that once, because you answered so quickly without any hesitation. You knew it, like you know now something, something is gonna change your world, indeed. "Boy," you said. "Boy."

And you clasped your hand on hers' and pushed in a little to feel a tiny, perfect foot. At that moment, you swore, nothing, nothing was ever going to harm your son.

You grab her hand and drag her toward the roof. She fights you, but adrenaline and your size win out, and you push her up the steps and onto the tarpaper.

Pools... sorrow, waves...joy.

It's already too late. The sky fills with light. Around you and your ex-wife, people scream in scrambled circles. Hairs on your arms and neck stand up and out. You run your tongue over dry fuzz on your teeth.

Danielle shakes you. You are shocked at her strength. You open your mouth to tell her, to tell her everything—but she is yelling a question at you. When she yells like that, she sounds and looks just like Danny.

"Where's Danny?" she yells. "Where's my daughter?"

Part Three: Seven Wonders

The adage "Practice makes perfect" has been generally accepted by Earth-English speaking cultures as a truism since its earliest publication as "*Uor wone maketh maister*" in the 1340 *Ayenbite of Inwyt.*

The *Ayenbite* was an Earth-Middle-English translation of the even earlier Earth-French treatise on Earth-Christian-religious-morality, *Somme le Roi*, so the saying may even, in actuality, be older and more deeply embedded in the Earth-Western subconscious than realized by linguists and historians.

Unsurprisingly, the adage loses all legitimacy when applied to the Ooya landing of a retrieval agent.

Alien arrivals would not have been on the minds of the Benedictine monks whose dutiful copying brought the saying into popular use. And indeed, the saying was valid when applied to Earth-ventures such as playing the trumpet or learning a language or catching a football, for no matter how many times the Trainer ran Natalie through touchdown procedures, Natalie's actual appearance at 3:30 AM, sitting on a bus stop bench in the heart of San Francisco, might be deemed inelegant but acceptable by a bystander, but disappointingly amateurish and dangerously perceptible by her Trainer.

Worse, the landing left Natalie thoroughly nauseated. She held her supply pack against her stomach, ducked her head between her legs, and threw up.

Her eyes adjusted as she wiped her mouth, and she realized she wasn't alone. A woman sat next to her on the bench. She was significantly taller than Natalie, who was designed to be on the average-small size of adult humans, with larger-than-average eyes, to encourage hormonal release of oxytocin in surrounding humans who would, hopefully want to protect and help her. Maybe six feet tall, Natalie thought, judging by how much further out the woman's boots were planted in front and how deeply the woman bent over between own her knees, also throwing up, as if in solidarity.

The woman's pile of vomit, watery and pink compared to Natalie's syrupy gray, indicated that the woman probably hadn't seen Natalie's arrival. The smell of ethanol rising from the vomit—potato-based vodka?—implied that even if she had seen, it more than likely hadn't registered as anything stranger than anything else.

The woman turned her head, still between her knees, to look at Natalie, but as she did, Natalie could swear—a contact drunk, if such was possible?—the woman's hair was slipping off. But it was, a swell of crinkly yellow hair sliding off the woman's head. With maybe six millimeters to spare above the vomit, before she could process why someone's hair would slip off their head as they threw up, Natalie caught it. As soon as she touched it, she understood—it was a wig—and she was relieved and pleased her reflexes were intact.

The woman threw up some more, then sat up. Under the streetlight, the woman's makeup was smeared, stubble shadowed her Adam's apple, and the soft tissue around one eye was bruised and swelling. Then, remembering, she snatched the wig from Natalie angrily and plopped it crookedly over her black and silver crew-cut like it was a child who wouldn't stop fidgeting. "This wig was five hundred dollars," she snapped at Natalie.

She didn't say anything about Natalie's high-speed grab. "I saved it," Natalie replied.

The woman studied Natalie. Natalie had saved it. The woman's anger softened at the little woman with the big eyes holding a backpack to her stomach in front of a pile of gray vomit. "Honey," she said to Natalie. "What did you eat?"

"Protein shake," Natalie said.

The woman shook her head. "What happened to you?"

"I had a hard landing," Natalie said.

"Love it," the woman said. She smiled and gave a little laugh. "So did I."

Lights floated by. A car. It drove slowly past them and halfway past, went dark.

The woman looked scared. No, mad. No, something. Natalie tried to read her, but all the woman did was watch the car, then lick the corners of her mouth and wince like she tasted something bad. "This is not a great neighborhood for either of us," she said as the car disappeared around the block. "Can you stand?" The woman barely looked like she could stand herself, but she pushed herself up with one hand, the other holding the wig. She was even taller than Natalie had estimated. She hadn't taken into consideration the platforms on the boots, which added at least another four inches.

"I can stand," Natalie said. She stood awkwardly. Although she'd practiced causal conversations until she was certified fluent, again, practice didn't make perfect, and she had no idea what to say next.

"What's your name, honey?" the woman asked.

Natalie was relieved. She could answer that. "Natalie."

The woman seemed delighted. "My sister's name is Natalie," she said.

It didn't surprise Natalie. It was the 14th most popular name in the Earth-United States. That was why it had been chosen for her. "About 1 in every 223 women in the United States of America is named Natalie," Natalie responded.

"Still," the woman said. "I am partial to Natalies." As the car materialized at the beginning of the block again, the woman grabbed Natalie's arm and started walking, dragging Natalie with her. The woman took long strides until they'd covered two blocks and there were more people out on the street. When she stopped, Natalie stopped next to her. "By the way," she said. "I'm Stevie." She whirled around so her skirt puffed out. "Like Stevie Nicks. See it now?"

Natalie didn't know what she should be seeing, but she tried a smile. Now that they had exchanged names, she knew a smile was customary.

"Which way are you headed, Natalie?"

"I don't know," Natalie said. "I'm supposed to find someone."

"You're too old to be a runaway," Stevie said. "Are you a traveler?"

"Traveler?"

"You know. Hitching rides, riding the rails, staying where ever. Fighting the power. Rejecting the man."

"I'm not looking for a man," Natalie said.

"Good for you, honey." Stevie touched her arm. "I don't suppose you have a place to stay while you look for this person, do you?"

"No."

"Before I take you home, then, we should get to know each other." Stevie's voice suddenly deepened. "My name is Steven Parsons. I'm 42 years old and I do this professionally, although..." Stevie touched her swollen eye. "I think I'm on vacation until this heals."

"You do this professionally?"

Stevie spun around again. "I'm Stevie Nicks, professionally. At clubs and shows and parties. Wherever. Las Vegas. The 'Night of a Thousand Stevies,' ooh, I'm doing that again this year." Stevie looked at Natalie. "Anyway, I've lived in San Francisco my whole life, and I live alone if you don't count my sister Natalie's stuff. She's in the army and stays with me sometimes, but mostly, I pay rent for her stuff."

Natalie understood all of Stevie's words, but the context was too complicated. But she smiled again and nodded until she realized Stevie was waiting for her to talk. "My name is Natalie Mitchell," she said, just as she'd rehearsed. Mitchell was the 44th most popular name on the continent, and the two names fit together nicely. "I'm 22 years old and I'm a...traveler. This is my first night here."

Stevie grabbed Natalie's hand and shook it up and down. Then she dropped Natalie's hand and grabbed her shoulder, as if what she was going to say was of grave importance. "Tell me, Natalie. You don't have a weapon or a knife or anything you can kill me with in that backpack of yours?"

"I have nail clippers in my hygiene kit."

Stevie laughed at that, and they started to walk again. Stevie was relaxed, still taking long strides, but now graceful, picking at the ground like a deer with suede hooves Natalie had spent a lot of time studying Earth-mammals. Her education had mostly been "need to know," but the Trainer encouraged her to learn everything. No one could predict what she would need to know for her mission.

"Aren't you going to ask me if I'm a serial killer or taking you home to attack you or something?" Stevie asked.

Natalie had also practiced self-defense, master level in Ooya fighting arts and human vulnerabilities (groin, neck, eye orbitals). "I could take you down, if necessary," Natalie answered.

Stevie laughed again. This was three times. There was scientific evidence that if a human laughed kindly at something another human said three times, then bonding had taken place. "That's the spirit," Stevie said.

Steve Parsons lived in an old, clean, third-story walk-up. It was stuffed with mismatched furniture, all pleasantly worn, and framed photos covering all available wall space. Natalie could sleep on the velvet couch, if she wanted. "Better for your back than you think," Stevie said, then corrected herself: "You're 22. Everything is fine for your back."

Natalie placed her pack on the couch and ran her hands along the back. It was soft, furry like an animal, but too cold and slow moving to be alive. She liked the way it felt.

A wooden head stood on a table by the door. Stevie draped the wig over it, straightened it, then stood back to admire the effect as if it were art. "It's all human hair, you know," she said. She rubbed the stiff silver hairs on her head, thinking. "I'm going to shower. You can take one too, if you want. Then I'll scramble us eggs. Make yourself at home." Then she said, "Ooh," remembering something, and pointed behind her, left, "Back there is my room," then center, "the bathroom," and right; "and the locked room is my sister's. You see the living room and kitchen. That's about the whole of my little palace. You want to shower, too, right?"

"I would like to wash," Natalie said. Stevie saluted her, then disappeared into the bathroom.

Natalie unzipped her pack while Stevie showered. She'd rehearsed with training packs, but this one was hers. Everything smelled new and still slightly like Ooya. Natalie was surprised she didn't feel sad at the smell. She'd learned about being homesick, only she wasn't. She looked at her hygiene pack: a brush for her mouth, a brush for her hair, and a small stick of perfumed jelly for under her arms. A double set of everything she was currently wearing now, plus a stiff little jacket, one gown to sleep in—with matching shoes—and one to dress up in, all in shades of sand and the same soft gray of a protein shake. A bag of currency. A communicator. And the source of the Ooya smell, a small feather her Trainer must have slipped in the bottom for Natalie to find.

Natalie traced the feather over her face. It was dangerous to have anything from home. Her Trainer taught her that. It was a small rebellion to include the feather. Natalie tried to recall other instances of rebellion by her Trainer, who'd tended her since gametogenesis. There was not a single one, until this.

Natalie couldn't just destroy the gesture. It meant something, although she did not know what. She outlined her lips with the feather, then placed it halfway down her throat and swallowed it.

It didn't go down well. It seemed stuck, halfway down her esophagus. It made her voice husky as she clicked on the communicator and whispered the Ooya word for "safe." She clicked the communicator off and shoved it back down into the bottom of her pack.

Stevie was finishing up. The air became warm and moist as she cracked the door while toweling off. Natalie looked at the photos that covered the wall while she waited. The images were all the same woman, with crinkly yellow hair much like the wig, soft brown eyes, and a button nose. In nearly every image, the woman was clad in gowns or robes the same texture as Stevie's couch.

Stevie appeared behind Natalie, a towel wrapped around her waist and head. "Yes," she said. "Those are all Stevie Nicks."

"You love her," Natalie said. The group of photos, when she realized they were all the same, struck her as a shrine.

"I do love her," Stevie said, sitting on the edge of the couch, almost on top of Natalie's pack. "Sometimes I think more than anyone. Except my sister." Stevie rubbed the towel on her head vigorously. "Although my parents are the ones who first bought me 'Rumours.'"

Natalie understood the word, but didn't grasp how rumors could be bought. There was so much she didn't know. She carried her nightgown into the room where Stevie had showered and played around with the knobs and levers until warm, clear water streamed down. Natalie stepped into the water and tried not to be afraid.

The Elders could have pulled out fear when they designed the experiments and the agents. But they chose not to. Fear, her Trainer explained, was a fine feature the Elders felt they couldn't improve upon. It developed over millions of years in the original human species as a way to deal with danger. Fear was an alert system. It released hormones and fat stores for energy and strength. It told humans to do something different than they were doing. In this case, though, Natalie was doing exactly what she was supposed to and still was afraid. But all she could do was swallow some sips of her shower water to force the feather further down her throat, dry off with a towel Stevie provided, and slip into her nightgown, crisp with newness and sharp folds.

Back in the main room, Stevie had put on music and started frying something in a pan. The noises were nice and the smells fatty and salty, and she told Stevie so.

"The eggs are just scrambled," Stevie said. "And the music is 'Rumours.'"

"Rumours," Natalie answered. One puzzle solved. The music was the rumor.

"Which song is your favorite on this?" Stevie asked, flipping over yellow patties in the pan.

"This one," Natalie said. Why not, she thought. The sounds were nice.

"'You Make Loving Fun'?" Stevie asked. She clucked her tongue and spooned out the yellow patties onto plates. "I, of course, prefer ones where Stevie Nicks sings rather than Christine McVie. 'Gold Dust Woman' is my favorite." Stevie brought over a plate, a fork, and a mug of clear yellow "chamomile tea," as she explained it. Natalie didn't like the tea, but the eggs were delicious, full of the fat she smelled and a good jolt of protein to replace what she had vomited. She recognized the taste from the training simulator. "Oh," Natalie said. "Chicken eggs."

"Indeed, honey. I hate those dyed egg whites full of chemicals." Stevie nodded. "Eat, then we'll sleep. Tomorrow, since I'm on…vacation, I'll help you find whoever you are looking for."

And Natalie chewed and smiled for the second time since landing on Earth.

Stevie poked Natalie awake with a gentle finger. He offered her two blue tablets and a cup of water. Natalie looked at her—Stevie's swollen eye was violet and dry-looking—then at the tablets, the water, and understood that Stevie wanted her to swallow them, but couldn't identify what the tablets were by sight. She raised one eyebrow, glad the gesture she'd practiced for so many hours in front of a training mirror was coming in handy.

"Naproxen," Stevie said. "If you feel like me, you've got a massive headache this morning."

Natalie felt fine, but she swallowed the pills dutifully. Naproxen inhibited selected coenzymes; it wouldn't hurt her to take. As soon as she swallowed, Stevie took back the water and looked at her.

"One other thing, honey," she said. "Close the curtain all the way around the tub next time you shower? The floor this morning was a little...wet."

That solved another puzzle, one she'd barely acknowledged the previous night. She'd assumed the curtain was ornamental: the whole bathroom was tiled and appeared to be waterproof. She'd never trained with a curtain in a bathroom. She tried to see how apologetic she needed to be, how big of a misstep it was, but Stevie was already onto another subject: Natalie's skin.

Stevie had put down the water glass and held one of Natalie's wrists in her big hand. She was stroking the soft skin on the back of Natalie's arm. "Your skin," she said, "is just so lovely. It's perfect, like a baby's. Like you've never seen hard work or a hard night or pollution or smoked or anything. No wonder you don't wear make-up." Stevie gently placed Natalie's hand into Natalie's lap. "If I looked like you, I wouldn't either."

"Thank you," Natalie said, although it was not something for which she could take credit. The Elders worked hard on skin. Earlier generations of experiments wound up with unexpected imperfections—or the opposite: discernible, suspicious perfection—and a few, like the experiment Natalie's mission was to locate and secure, suffered from both imperfection and perfection. Natalie's own skin was grown from actual human cells. But Stevie was right; it was the skin of a baby's, for all intents and purposes.

"Are you hungry? Stevie asked. She was already in the kitchen, opening cabinets, obviously hungry herself. "I can make us something, and then we can get started on finding your friend."

Friend. Natalie chewed over the word as she chewed on the toast and marmalade Stevie placed in front of her. Was Kizzy a friend? Natalie had never met her, specifically, but grew up in her shadow, studying her, monitoring her. From the time she was a child, even with accelerated growth, Natalie knew she'd been created to locate and secure her, an early-generation immersion experiment. She knew her, but was she a friend?

Natalie looked up at Stevie, who was already heaping her plate with more toast and filling a mug with hot coffee. Natalie held the mug to her nose; the coffee smelled like what the Earth-forest simulator had puffed out, all acidic dirt and plant oils released by rain. She liked it, and two heaping spoonfuls of sugar made her like it even more. She stirred the coffee until it cooled and the smell weakened. *No*, she thought. *Stevie is my friend. Kizzy is my mission.*

"Tell me who we're looking for," Stevie said.

"Her name is Kizzy," Natalie said.

"A girlfriend!" Stevie smiled at that, marmalade slick on her teeth.

"Not a girlfriend." Natalie swallowed the last of her coffee. "But I've known her all my life."

"And she's in San Francisco?"

"I don't know," Natalie admitted. "She could be. Or anywhere within 1,700 kilometers." That was as precise as tracking could point.

"Kilometers?" Stevie said. "I don't know how far that is. But it sounds like a lot."

"The planet is more than 40,000 kilometers around," Natalie pointed out.

"When you put it like that, I guess 1,700 kilometers does narrow it down." Stevie sighed. "You have no idea where this Kitty is."

"Kizzy," Natalie said. Within 1,700 kilometers had felt entirely feasible, considering how far she'd even had to travel to simply get on the planet. But Stevie's face looked dubious, and so Natalie answered, "I guess I don't."

"You know her last name, though, right? You said you've known her your whole life."

Natalie nodded.

"The Internet, then!" Stevie rubbed her hands over her chin. "I have to shave," she interjected, then continued, "If she's your age, then she's on whatever you kids are using these days."

"Yes, OK," Natalie said. She hadn't practiced with Internet, but she'd read about the planet-wide network and studied Earth-English-speaking films where characters used the Internet to communicate, look up information, or view photos of other humans in the nude. "Do you have a terminal I can access?'

"Why, yes," Stevie answered. "I have a 'terminal' you can access in my room." She giggled. "You are a funny little thing, you know that? You have a funny little sense of humor."

Natalie was happy with that. Humor was a desirable, admired quality among humans and, she realized, not a terrible disguise for Natalie's knowledge gaps. "Thank you," she answered.

"You mind much if I rehearse while you work?" Stevie said. "If it bothers you, you can close the bedroom door. I won't be insulted." Something about the way she said it suggested that she would indeed be injured if Natalie closed the door, a sign of aversion and rejection, and Natalie determined to keep the door open, no matter what kinds of sounds or smells or lights emerged while Stevie rehearsed whatever she was going to rehearse.

Stevie walked Natalie into her room; enormous unmade bed, hand-painted vanity with a three-way mirror, a small desk with a laptop-style personal computer and some stacked books, the redolence of many nights of breathing through a human mouth. She tapped the computer to life with a few keystrokes, "My password is 'Belladonna,'" and then Natalie was in the small chair at the small desk, alone, trying to determine what she should do next.

Letter keys on the keyboard typed out letters in the order tapped, she learned. A small blank pad tracked an arrow around the screen. Hitting the pad with a fingertip activated something beneath the arrow, but only sometimes. She was puzzled until she realized some objects lit up slightly while others did not, and she could tap the lit objects. She pushed herself away from the desk. She had to ask what to use to search for Kizzy, and decided if she asked with a smile, Stevie might think she was being humorous again, which was acceptable, as long as she also got the information she needed. As she moved toward the door, music swelled from the living room again, like it had the previous night, but different sounds to the music, a song she had never heard.

The singing started, the same voice that Stevie had identified as Stevie Nicks' the night before. Stevie herself began singing along, matching her tone and pitch to Stevie Nicks', deep and raspy, smooth and a little hoarse.

"So long ago..." the two Stevies sang, and Stevie tossed her head as if she were wearing her long, crinkly wig.

Natalie leaned against the wall. If she watched Stevie, she missed the lyrics, if she closed her eyes to concentrate, she couldn't see. She did both, getting a few seconds of Stevie, then a few seconds of words: *live to see the seven wonders.*

It was beautiful and sad.

"Was I bothering you?" Stevie asked, pleased at Natalie's sadness.

"No," Natalie answered. "It was lovely."

"It's a new song for me." Stevie said.

"I wish I had time to see the seven wonders." Natalie sighed. She was jealous, and said so.

"Oh, I've never seen them. It's just the song," Stevie said. "I think I learned about them in school. One of them was a garden. And the big pyramid in Egypt."

Natalie was surprised. There were several sets of seven Earth-wonders, grouped together as pinnacles of human achievement and creativity. They seemed like things humans would know about, if not flock to. "There are the wonders of the ancient world. The hanging gardens of King Nebuchadnezzar II in Babylon, the Giza pyramid, a lighthouse in Alexandria, the Mausoleum of Mausso—"

"Yes, those," Stevie interrupted, shaking her head. "You must be awesome at trivia nights, honey." She wasn't interested in the seven wonders, which baffled Natalie, since she had just sung so passionately about them. "How's the search coming?"

"I don't know how to find her."

"Want my help?" Stevie assumed the answer was affirmative, because she was already in her room and at her desk before Natalie had a chance to answer. "What's her name again?"

"Kizzy," Natalie answered. "Kizzy Jeneko. With a J"

Stevie tapped at the computer, sucking on her lower lip. "Nothing." She tapped again. "Nothing. Wait. Here's a blog with an entry that talks about a Kizzy. It belongs to Roxana Jeneko. From Seattle. That's about 800 miles. Is that the same as 1500 kilometers?"

"1700. And yes," Natalie answered.

"Does your Kizzy have a sister?"

"She might."

Stevie kept tapping at the keys, then whistled. "Check her out. Yowza."

An image opened on the screen: a young woman with reddish black hair, twisted and pinned in a complicated style. Her skin was the color of Stevie's coffee, dilute with cream, and her eyes stared right out at Natalie, so dark it was impossible to discern between iris and pupil.

"Pretty, right?" Stevie said, practically whistling. She clicked again, and another image formed on the screen, the same woman, in a long dress and headscarf, sitting in an orange chair built into a wood-grain wall. In the bottom right hand corner, almost out of frame, was a pink hand, the fingers squared off as if they'd been manicured that way.

They weren't, of course. They were designed, before the Elders knew the subtle irregularities of natural humans—the lack of symmetry, the ratio of features and proportion.

Kizzy. She was in Seattle.

"Yes," Natalie said. "That must be her sister."

Stevie tapped again: the same woman, in a bar, beer tipped back to her mouth; perceptibly older with cropped hair and baggy cargo shorts, feet planted shoulder-width apart against a backdrop of dark trees and haze. "And this Roxana's a dyke. How wonderful!" Stevie said. "Don't look at me like that. I have excellent gaydar. Not always for me—" she said, touching her eye, "—but dykes I can spot at 50 yards. Whatever that is in kilometers." Stevie looked at Natalie. "Although with you, I didn't know right away."

"Know what?"

"That you're family. Until you told me 'no men.' And then I saw your clothes." Stevie clicked her tongue. "You know, you should try femme. It would suit you." She got up excitedly. "Some jewelry and scarves. Accessories make the outfit, you know."

Natalie slid into the desk chair and started tapping the image like Stevie had. She mimicked Stevie's movements, and the images changed, changed, changed, all without any Kizzy, until the images cycled back to the first one again with her twisted, knotted hair.

"I bet she has an email. You should email her."

Natalie understood. Email referred to electronic mail. A form of personal communication conducted via the Internet. "I have never emailed."

Stevie stopped her pacing and stared at Natalie. Then she laughed. "God, your sense of humor is so strange." Then she straightened her face. "You're serious. You have no email."

"I have no email."

Stevie waved at her to move out of the chair. "We need to get you one. Right this second." She tapped furiously. "What do you want your address to be. Your name?" She tapped again. "Natalie is taken, of course." She tapped, then bit a nail. "And so is Natalie Mitchell. You have a middle name?"

"No," Natalie said. The Elders didn't think middle names were necessary. Sociological studies demonstrated that middle names were getting less and less common in the Earth-United Sates, with the exception of mothers attaching their surnames, or their mothers' surnames, to their baby's names. She needed a name, though, something that would distinguish her from the approximately 274,000 humans named Natalie and the 145,540 humans with the surname Mitchell. "How about Emmiline? Like the song?"

Stevie slapped the desk with pleasure. "Perfect." She tapped a few more times, then scooted back from the desk. There you go. Your new email. Now send a message to this Roxana."

Natalie sat at the desk, fingers poised over the letter keys.

"Introduce yourself. Tell her you found her blog."

"Should I tell her I'm looking for Kizzy?"

"Not if you want to get in her pants."

Natalie did not understand at first why she would want inside Roxana's pants, but then, once she thought about it, it made sense. Being in her shoes, in her pants. In her place, near Kizzy. "All right," Natalie said. "Should I tell her I want in her pants?"

Stevie laughed at that. "Do not tell her you want in her pants, if you want in her pants." She patted Natalie's shoulder. "Ah, shit. Don't listen to me. Just be yourself. I'll leave you to it. I'm going to rehearse again."

Natalie ran her fingers over the letters on the keyboard, as the seven wonders song started again.

She would just be herself. Her fingers curled into claws, then relaxed. She tapped at the COMPOSE button, and a white rectangle opened on the screen. She liked that. It sounded like she was going to write a song. Then she tapped at a letter, and it appeared behind the blinking line in the rectangle. A few more taps showed that the long bar at the bottom gave spaces between words. "My name is Natalie," she said, as she typed. "I am 22 and a traveler. My friend Stevie Parsons and I found your blog online." She thought for a second. "Your skin is like Stevie's coffee, dilute with cream." She watched the blinking line on the screen, then typed, "I would like to meet you." Then she tapped the button labeled SEND, and the rectangle folded up and disappeared, replaced with a button that said, 'Your email has been sent.'

Done, she pushed back out of the chair and lay down on Stevie's bed. She was exhausted by the effort. The last thing she remembered was the song beginning again.

When Natalie woke, the light was blue with sunset. Stevie lay next to her on the bed, whistling slightly as she breathed, hands folded against her flat, stubbly chest. Natalie rolled onto her side, facing Stevie, to watch her sleep.

Stevie whistled again, then snorted awake. "Hi," she said. She stretched out, rolled onto her back, and scratched the longish hairs that curled around one dark pink nipple.

"I always think of you as female," Natalie said. "But you really aren't."

"It's because you met me in drag, probably. But, no, I am definitely not female," Stevie said. "Although I am pretty feminine." Stevie touched his eye, which seemed slightly less purple and more brown. "I don't really care how you think of me, though. I'm just me. Always have been. It's all just socially constructed anyway. You don't mind I joined you, do you? Looked so comfortable. And I always used to take naps with my sister."

Natalie didn't mind. She realized she actually liked it, as well as the easy intimacy of talking in bed, her mouth dry with sleep, the mingled smells of her and her friend, Stevie. "Tell me about your sister?"

Stevie sat up. "Another time," he said. "I'll tell you about my Natalie another time." He stood up. He was wearing thin boxer shorts, and Natalie could see his gluteal muscles through the fabric. "Are you hungry?" he asked. "I'm hungry."

"I am." She rose herself. Her clothes were wrinkled from lying in them, but the fabric smoothed with a few tugs.

"Ooh!" Stevie said, tying the sash of his bathrobe. "Check your email. See if that hottie has replied." He stood behind the chair and tapped at the computer. "She has! Can I read it?"

Natalie nodded, and Stevie started tapping again before she could complete one full cycle of chin up, chin down. "She wants a picture!" He smiled at Natalie. "Of course she does. We should slut you up a bit."

Natalie didn't understand what he meant, but she grinned. The mission was going better than she expected, better than her Trainer had prepared her for. She'd already made successful contact with someone close to Kizzy. Social convention called for celebration at times like these, and she immediately appreciated the practice. She wanted to celebrate. She was rich with currency; she should take Stevie out. "Let's go somewhere. A restaurant to celebrate. I will pay. I have currency."

"Yes!" Stevie moved towards her in a sashay-type dance. "Let's dress up, and I can take your picture before we go."

This time, Natalie showered first. She closed the curtain tightly around her and looked up into the stream of water. She hadn't yet felt rain and wondered if this was what it was like.

She dried herself, and as Stevie showered, she rubbed the stick of jelly under her arms, brushed her hair, and slipped into her gown with the matching soft little shoes. She turned her communicator on and then off again; she wasn't sure what she wanted to report. She wasn't ready to tell the Elders she'd located Kizzy, because, logically, she really hadn't yet. She turned it on again and instead reported she was still safe and in acclimation and talked a little about Stevie using first the feminine form, then the masculine. An Elder immediately sent back a question about Stevie, and Natalie tried to find an Ooya word to describe her friend. As she was thinking, the Elder sent down an inquiry, an image of an Earth-based clown-performer, in full makeup with a big, round, red nose and a pointed, polka-dotted hat.

Stevie was not a clown. Natalie learned that this was not a positive image, and was angry and hurt at the implication.

She hissed, "No," in Ooya, and slammed the communicator off. She knew the Elders would have more questions, especially about her response. They would find it interesting. On Ooya, things are what they are, and there is nothing hurtful or anger-making about it. The Elders are a people of science, and they would want her to explain. Instead, Natalie shoved the communicator down into her pack like it was the thing that had hurt and angered her.

Stevie came in, smelling clean and a little like mint. He'd painted over his eye a little, to camouflage the purple, although it still looked puffier than the other eye. He had on blue jeans and thick-soled boots, but the tailored jacket he wore over his tight black t-shirt made him looked formal, polished. He considered her, in her long, gray dress and flat shoes, and clicked his tongue. "Sit down at the table," he said.

Natalie sat down and waited for him to return with a covered, handled box. Opened, the box gave off a sweet, powdery smell, and Stevie instructed Natalie to close her eyes.

A soft brush tickled her eyelids, then puffed over her nose. She sneezed from the fine dust. Stevie's tongue poked from the side of his mouth as he dabbed and swabbed her with different sponges and things. "Now, open your mouth wide."

Natalie did, and he slicked something over her lips. It had the same consistency as her underarm jelly.

"Rub your lips together and then smack," he instructed and demonstrated. She imitated his movement and the jelly made her lips feel stiff and sticky.

"Yes," he said. "You need something...else, though." He studied her, hand over his mouth. He disappeared into a back room, and Natalie heard a series of thumps. He re-emerged with a length of material. He motioned for her to stand up, and he laid the material, a blue scarf, its weave large, its drape heavy, once around her neck, then into an X over her chest. The material was soft and papery, and a small embroidered tag informed her that it was 100% linen.

"My sister picked that up in Italy. She barely ever wore it, which is a pity," he said. "It's perfect. You look perfect." He steered her by the shoulders into the bathroom and aimed her at the mirror.

Natalie barely recognized herself. Dark gray lined her eyes, making them even larger than they actually were, and her lips had the light pink sheen of a pearl. The scarf made her clothes look both planned and carefree, and the blue set off her dark hair in a way she could never have imagined.

"Now, turn to me," he said. He had his phone up and pointed at her. "The light's great in here." The phone clicked. "Smile a little," he instructed. "Show some teeth." He smiled. "Perfect! Let's send this one to her," he said, showing Natalie the tiny screen. "Love it."

Natalie developed a routine.

She would wake up, always earlier than Stevie, and attempt to reproduce the scrambled eggs he'd served her on the first night. Then, she'd walk around the city while Stevie rehearsed, then come back and email Roxy to describe everything she'd seen: knock-kneed surfers paddling around Ocean Beach, tall ships swaying in the Aquatic Park docks, the fortified buildings and sand dunes in the Presidio, the sweeping views from the top of Telegraph Hill. Then, she napped alongside Stevie, and when they woke up, they ate dinner, or, sometimes, saw a movie or watched television. Other times, Stevie snuck her into his performances. "I do not know how you even exist without ID," Stevie told her, as he led her into the back door of a dressing room at a club in the Mission. "You need a driver's license for everything. Get into clubs, drink. Hell, I don't even know how you traveled. You need ID to travel."

Natalie understood, in that moment, how terribly she was trained for this mission. Her Trainer emphasized some things and not others, taught her nothing about the basics. She knew history, but not culture; biology, but not health.

But she learned. She learned about Stonewall and Cher, mojitos and Thai food. She loved being on Earth and being young. She loved music and poured through Stevie's collection—every Fleetwood Mac, Stevie Nicks, and Lindsey Buckingham album ever made, along with a good collection of '70s hard rock, bass-dense dance and dubstep, and a little flamenco jazz. When Stevie described her as dancing "like you're from outer space," she'd giggle, and keep going. Natalie's response to any references to space usually involved giggles. She giggled at science fiction movies that involved aliens, alien invasion, and first contact, as well as political discussions about the status of "illegal aliens," although she never explained herself to Stevie. One night, after one more mojito than she was used to, she almost told him, but it was as if the feather was, again, in her throat, and so she didn't say a word, only giggled.

She loved to giggle.

But most of all, she loved emails from Roxy, and then her phone calls with Roxy. She'd walk away from them singing snippets of songs she'd come to love, like "Seven Wonder," the sticky beats of "Slow Ride," the frenzied pain of the crescendo in "Free Bird," or the wailing vocals of "Magic Man."

Roxy talked about the woods where she worked and the quiet of her job, as well as about her family—her father and mother, uncle and aunt, grandmother—and, of course, her sister. One night, on video chat, Roxy sang to Natalie an old gypsy folk song until Natalie started, uncontrollably, to cry.

After that, Natalie could only think of Roxy's gentle grin when Natalie had begged her, wiping away tears with the edge of the Italian linen scarf, to keep on singing. She found herself telling Roxy not about what she saw, but other things, things she felt and carried around like that slow smile: worrying over fragile-looking birds scrapping for crumbs in the park; holding the thin, cold hand of an old woman to help her across the street; interrogating a street preacher about the idea of a soul. She told her about the breezes from the west, carrying the smell of brine and fish into the open windows of the apartment, and the thrilling crack and flesh-shaking boom of the fireworks on Independence Day. And when Roxy explained she couldn't tell anyone in her family, except her sister, about Natalie, Natalie understood. She did not mention Roxy in her reports back to Ooya. Instead, she described surfing and historical military campuses and streets that required stairs to climb, and she patiently answered their follow-ups, even when the cold logic of the Elders' questions upset her.

The Elders were a people of science, and she had been created for science, for knowledge, just as the Ooya were themselves designed and created as servants, gathering knowledge for the Minds. She was created as a follow-up to their Earth experiments, whose research cycle was coming to an end. The Ooya were passionately interested in how a small planet could develop such a diversity of life—life that flies, swims, walks—of carbon and oxygen, nitrogen and calcium, and just a few others. Such a small set of elements to create everything around her. To create a beautiful woman who sang to her.

As soon as Stevie explained mix tapes, Natalie wanted to make one for Roxy. She spent two straight days squatting prostrate before Stevie's stereo, mixing and erasing a two-hour interlude. At hour 26, Stevie made her down a milkshake for strength, musing how, truly, nothing hurt Natalie's young, strong back. The truth was, her back was starting to hurt, quite a bit, and she kept herself going by swallowing more of Stevie's blue Naproxen pills from behind the bathroom mirror. She'd been told by her Trainer that aging would be perceptible, but it had been abstract until these days passed under the weight of gravity. They were different, knowing and understanding, and her back and knees taught her the divergence between them.

When the mix was complete, Stevie mailed it to Roxy for her.

The following week Natalie could hear it playing in the background as she spoke to Roxy on the phone. She mouthed along with the lyrics: *And this bird you cannot change.*

"My uncle," Roxy said, "My mother's older brother is getting married in Florida next week. Again. My parents gave Kizzy and me permission to drive down there, just the two of us."

Lord knows, I can't change.

"And, I'd like to stop along the way and see you," Roxy continued.

Lord, I can't… Natalie stopped mouthing in the middle of the line. "With your sister?" Her voice shook, but only a little.

Roxy didn't seem to notice. "I want to tell Kiz. I think she can handle it."

"To clarify, I'll get to meet you and Kizzy?" Natalie asked.

Roxy laughed. “Yes. Is that OK with you? Would that be OK with your friend?”

“I will have to ask, but I predict he will be pleased with additional company.” Natalie sat back in the chair. She said her good-byes to Roxy and, as she hung up, was suddenly exhausted. It was an hour before their customary nap, but Natalie wrapped herself in one of Stevie’s small blankets and lay down on the bed. The bed smelled now of equal parts Stevie and her. It was interesting to smell her own smell, since she rarely smelled herself as she moved through the day. She was glad her smell was, overall, a pleasant one, reminding her a little of medium-done toast and the acidic fruity scent of her underarm jelly.

She stirred as Stevie climbed in beside her, feeling as if she’d slept for hours already. She rolled over and closed her eyes, but Stevie touched her back. He wanted to talk. Usually he wanted to talk when they were waking up, blinking away the confusing weight of daytime sleep. She rolled back toward him.

He was sitting with his knees drawn up, chin resting on his hands. “I wanted to thank you,” he said. “To tell you how grateful I am that you came into my life when you did.” He was silent for a few seconds, but not to wait for her response. He continued, “I didn’t even realize how deeply I was in trouble. Sometimes, things are just meant to be.” He touched her arm. “So, thank you. Thank you for all the choices that led you to that bench that night. All those decisions that brought you into my life.”

He said other things, along the same line, but Natalie didn’t hear them. She began to cry. She had been placed on that bench, built for a mission that had nothing to do with Stevie. She’d never made a single decision. She hadn't even been herself for more than the equivalent of a year.

Vat-grown, her Trainer tended to her mitosis, then her respiration levels, adjusting the levels of nutrients by rate of growth. Her Trainer controlled her digestion and elimination of waste and monitored the pulses carving a childhood and adolescence of knowledge into her brain. Her Trainer even moved her joints as she tripled in size, combed her hair, and then cleaned the growth compound from her when she awoke, held and sang to her through the first days and nights, and oversaw her further education, always scanning for defects until the very hour of her departure.

"There you were. You just appeared like magic," Stevie said. "Named Natalie, of all things."

Yes, she'd chosen Natalie from the list of moderately popular Earth-English gendered names, pleased with the way each syllable forced open the mouth and with the trouble the Elders had with the soft a and e sounds. But that was it, her only decision, and even that from a set of carefully considered and limited options.

Stevie tried wiping away her tears with the side of his hand, but they dropped from her eyes too quickly. He pulled her in and held her to his chest. The little hairs tickled her nose, and so she calmed a little. But when she tried to pull away, he held her firmly in place.

"You wanted me to tell you about my sister," Stevie said. "I can do that now, if you want to hear."

She didn't need to hear. She heard it in his heartbeat. "She's dead, isn't she?" Natalie asked, surprised at herself that she read it.

Stevie nodded, and Natalie cried again. He peeled her cheek, gluey with salt, away from his chest and raised her face to his.

His eyes were a deep brown, with a cloudy blue ring around the outside of the iris. She'd never looked this deeply at him before; she didn't mind actual physical proximity, but examining him closely made her shy and uncomfortable. But he looked at her with no reservations; he held her chin so she couldn't squirm away.

"You know," he said. "You really are beautiful." He kissed her.

Kissing was a surprise. She'd prepared for this, of course, and the Elders had even designed a simulator for most physical situations. And she'd hugged and kissed her Trainer, but Ooya mouths were not human mouths, and it was more like running her lips over Steven's velvet sofa, and the simulator was not this hot or wet.

But then Natalie remembered what a kiss symbolized, what a kiss promised, and where it could lead. She pushed Stevie away hard.

"I have slept with women on occasion," he said, as if to explain, but that wasn't it.

He wasn't her mission. She couldn't back up or deliver or go to the kiss's promise. And as an image of Roxy came to her mind, she realized she didn't want to, either. "That's not it," she said.

He looked carefully at her, but this time, she didn't meet his eyes. It would have been painful to do so, and she instinctively, like all the others of her species, designed or born, avoided pain. He slumped back down on the bed and rolled onto his side so she faced his back.

She placed her hand on his hip. She'd made many decisions since she arrived on Earth. She didn't have any agency over her beginnings, but, who did? For better or worse, she'd decided to follow Steven Parsons home. She'd decided to trust him. In trusting him, she'd decided to allow him to trust her. All small calibrations and variations on what could have happened, all culminating onto this path, this moment, this awkward miscue.

But he wasn't her mission. Kizzy Jeneko was her mission.

"Roxana is coming here to meet me," Natalie said to Stevie's back. "She's bringing Kizzy."

"They're coming here?" he said into his pillow.

"Is that OK?"

He didn't answer. Instead, he lifted his head slightly. "Can I ask you a favor?" he asked. "Will you clean out Natalie's room? Keep what you want, throw the rest away. Donate it. There are charities that will come and pick up boxes." He turned and looked at her with one eye. "Will you do that for me?"

"Yes," Natalie answered. "I will do that for you."

He placed his head back down into the pillow.

"I'd be honored," she continued. She touched the back of his head. The stubble was sharp, but she pressed her palm down over his scalp. Then she sang him to sleep, the only song to which she knew the words, "Seven Wonders."

Natalie woke up, and something was different. The apartment was quiet. She sat up and crinkled the note Stevie had taped to her stomach.

Dearest Natalie, it read. *I'm off to do a few days in Vegas. Better if we have a few days of space. Give my love to Roxana and her sister. Love, Steven. Also, will you still do what you promised me?*

"I will," she assured the note. "I will do that."

She made eggs. She walked around the apartment, picking things up and putting them down again. She listened to the downstairs neighbor get ready for work. Then she poked around on Stevie's computer to find the number for this charity he'd mentioned, that would come and pick up boxes. They had an appointment calendar on their website, and she poked at it until it confirmed a pick up the next morning.

She stood outside Natalie's door for a few seconds before going inside. It felt respectful, somehow, to add some drama to the affair.

The room smelled dry and like a rotting orange. She traced the orange to a desiccated fruit carcass hung in the closet by a red ribbon. The sugars crumbled into powder in her hand.

The clothes were easy. There weren't many of them; a life mostly spent in uniform didn't require an extensive wardrobe.

The bookshelf was heavy with history textbooks, a complete Learn Spanish course, and a large portfolio of ornamental, deeply patterned art reproductions by Alfonse Maria Mucha. The computer wouldn't turn on, no matter how many times she tapped the keyboard.

Natalie bagged and boxed nearly everything, leaving a few things she thought Stevie would want. She folded the American flag tacked to the wall over the bed, and laid on top a wooden hairbrush, its bristles bound with hairs, a worn green leather wallet, and a cheaply framed image of a little boy, in red overalls. The boy had Stevie's eyes, and he struggled to hold up a bright pink infant—swaddled in brighter pink, and half the length of him—with all the gentleness and excitement of someone holding the crux of the world in their arms. It was a look of astonished, overwhelming love, and Natalie kept looking at the image, putting it down on top of the flag next to the hairbrush, then turning it back over to look at it again.

She'd seen that expression before: when she opened her eyes for the very first time in the arms of her Trainer.

The ringing phone startled her into realizing the sun had passed through the room. It was afternoon already.

Roxana spoke so quickly, Natalie asked her to repeat herself.

"Kizzy is sick," she said. "She gets like this sometimes. She'll be fine, but I should really take her back to Seattle. She can't go on like this, and I'd be cruel to make her."

Natalie kept silent to hide her disappointment. She'd set the cart, as the maxim went, before the horse—a quote, she silently noted to herself that, in its original form, "*Moche uolk ȝetteþ þe ȝuolȝ be-uore þe oksen*," or "Many folk set the plough before the oxen" was also taken from the *Ayenbite of Inwyt*. "It's OK," she finally said. "I understand."

When they hung up, Natalie sat on the floor and cried. Then she picked herself up and looked out the window at the skyline. She'd never felt this alone, ever, in her life. She finished Natalie's room, napped, and then paced. She went to the stereo and put on music to try to fill the space, but found herself clicking at her communicator.

"I would like to speak to my Trainer," she told the Elder.

"Explain," it answered her, flatly.

"Repeat," Natalie said, "My Trainer."

"Explain." The Elders had more patience than Natalie did. This could go on for hours.

"I miss her," she said, in Earth-English. There were no Ooya words that came close enough.

"Elaborate," the Elder said, and Natalie felt the tingle of scanner fingers walking up and down her body.

"Readings are normal," the Elder said, once the scan was complete. If Natalie didn't know better, she would have detected a note of surprise. "Report circumstances," the Elder continued.

"I want to speak to my Trainer," Natalie said. "I miss her and I need to talk with her."

"Your Trainer is tending other issue," another Elder said. Natalie could sense the change in the frequency of the voice. Up the chain of command. She felt another set of scanner fingers start to walk up her spine. "Elaborate with me."

"Retract," Natalie said in Ooya. "I am fine," and clicked off the communicator before the Elder could answer.

The phone took her again by surprise. Roxana whispered, so low she had to ask her to speak up. "My family," Roxana said, "are all going to the wedding. Do you want—I mean, can you—if you want, come up here?"

"To Seattle?" As soon as she asked, she felt stupid. "Of course. Yes."

"Are you sure?" Roxy asked.

"Are you?"

"I'm sure. I just want to make sure—" Roxy stopped. Natalie could tell she felt stupid now.

"Will Kizzy be there?"

"Yes," Roxy said. "I want to tell Kizzy about us. She's the only one who would understand."

"How should I get there?"

"The train is a beautiful ride," Roxy said. "Lots of countryside. And it's not too expensive."

"I'm OK with money," Natalie said. They'd never discussed finances. She liked the idea of a train ride. But she had no identification. She needed it for travel, Stevie had said.

Then she had the idea. "I'll do it," she said.

"You'll really come?"

"Of course."

"Phone me with your info. Of course, I'll pick you up."

There was a train the next afternoon, which arrived in Seattle almost exactly 24 hours from its departure. Natalie promised Roxy she'd be on that one. They made soft promises to one another, and then hung up.

It took Natalie almost an hour after that to actually hold the green wallet in her hand. It was shiny in places, where Natalie's fingertips had glazed it with her skin oils and where it had been scraped a bit from being shoved into pockets or bags. In a clear plastic window was a stiff card marked California Driver License. Against a turquoise background, Natalie Parsons smiled as if she knew a secret about the photo taker, echoed in two small duplicates on the right side of the card. Natalie's hair was dark and loosely pulled back, her nose wider than Natalie's own and lips slightly thinner, but marked with an age that would make her 26 now, a small stretch, feasible. She slipped the license down into her pack, next to her communicator.

That evening, Natalie tried to make the hours move faster. She listened to music and ate some pizza, cold from the refrigerator. She stacked Natalie's boxes for the morning pick-up and lay down onto the couch, more exhausted than she thought she'd be. It was hard to gauge her limits, when each day they grew imperceptibly tighter with age.

It was the one thing the Elders hadn't quite smoothed out; retrieval agents of her generation continued their accelerated aging for the first year after birth. Then, once the body caught up completely with their age, it leveled off to normal, as long as they were traveling at speeds less than the speed of light.

The day had worn her out. But as she closed her eyes, there was a communicator buzz in her ear. The Elders never initiated a call down unless there was an immediate reason. She clicked on the communicator to the hushed voice of her Trainer.

"Child, are you unwell?" she asked. The distance and technology drained the music from her voice, but Natalie could hear the insistence, the risk.

The love.

Her Trainer was an Ooya designed and built to love, but it didn't make her love matter any less.

"Mother," Natalie said. "What should I do?"

Her Trainer didn't ask what she meant, because her Trainer knew the very patterns of her brain. Her Trainer could run a few statistical scenarios and get the gist of all that could happen.

"Do what you can, child, and then come home," her Trainer said. She sent down a scanner finger, but only to touch the tip of Natalie's nose, just like she did when Natalie got a good score on an exam or had endured the early assayments. Then, the communicator clicked off and Natalie was back in San Francisco, in a dark apartment, surrounded by boxes.

Natalie wasn't good at dreaming yet. She'd been better when she was growing, with the voice of her Trainer pushing through the fleeting images, full of meaning, explaining them as many times as she needed. But since she'd been born, as it were, dreams frightened her more often than not, even when she couldn't remember them. And even then, on Ooya, she could curl into her Trainer, and it'd all go away.

Her dreams were how she knew that she had slept some: dreams of Stevie holding her in his lap like he had his sister, dreams of her Trainer delicately touching disks of cold pizza with her long, feathered fingers, dreams of twelfth-century monks singing Fleetwood Mac songs. And dreams of Roxana: Roxy turning into Kizzy, and then back again.

The doorbell rang, and three workers from the charity carried away almost all of Natalie Parson's life. She had a moment, in solidarity with Stevie, when she didn't want to see the two teenagers and fat middle-aged guy take away the boxes, but in the end, she let them, closed the door, and sat on the carpet for a long time.

Then her communicator buzzed—once, twice. That was the signal of an Elder-initiated call. "Attentive," Natalie said in Ooya.

"We have concluded your mission," it said, in vibrations so deep they hurt. The pain made Natalie sure she'd misheard.

"Repeat?"

"We have concluded your mission. Return pending. Details to follow."

She panicked. She was about to leave, to complete her mission—and meet her first love. "Why?"

"We have concluded your mission. The experiment exceeded parameters. Deficiencies detected." The frequency deepened. "Return pending. Details to follow."

"You can't do this," Natalie answered, in English.

"Explain."

Natalie winced at the vibrations; she kept her eyes closed as the scanner fingers paced up and down her stomach.

"Explain," the Elder repeated. They would repeat until she did.

"I have located the issue," she said in Ooya.

"Contact?" it asked. "Elaborate."

"Through her sister," she whispered. She didn't want to ever tell them about Roxy. It felt like a betrayal.

The scanner fingers moved along her scalp. The connection was silent, but still active; it buzzed in her teeth.

"Experiment parameters extended. Disregard abort message. Mission addendum: retrieve related human along with issue."

Tears streamed down her face. A scanner finger wiped one away, but without comfort. "You've got to be kidding," Natalie said.

"Experiment parameters extended. Disregard abort message. Mission addendum: retrieve related human along with issue," it repeated.

"I can't. I won't."

"Report circumstances."

"It's wrong," she said. She didn't even know how to explain why. "I won't do it."

There was no response on the active line. The Elders were conferring. But then the scanner finger poked down the side of her face. It tweaked her nose. Then it clicked off.

Natalie lay back on the carpet. She wouldn't do it. She would stay here. No, she would get her own place. She'd find some work. She'd become a person.

Always on the run, but a person. She reached into her pack to grab her communicator. She'd destroy it. Then—

The feather in her throat moved. It grew. She coughed, choked a little as it stretched. The shaft filled the hollow in her spine, soft barbs creeping behind her nose, like a trapped sneeze, and into the corners of her eyes. By the time they reached into her brain, she could barely hear her own voice say, "I am sorry, child. This was how I could bring you home to me."

Natalie folded her spare clothes, her dress and shoes, her now-soft night gown, and her hygiene pack, amended since landing to include a light pink lip gloss and a pencil that left soft gray lines around her eyes, both purchased by Stevie as gifts to her, as well as a small chunk of amber resin tucked into a carved wooden box. The amber was one of the only two things Natalie had purchased for herself, the other a blue t-shirt screened with the San Francisco skyline from a tourist shop, and before slipping them down into her pack, she turned both of them over in her hands like she'd never seen them. She checked her currency bag, her communicator, an ID card with her name on it, and placed, on top of all of it, a blue linen scarf.

The note was hardest to leave. She sat looking at the blank backside of Stevie's note, trying to decide what to say.

She had a strange thought she didn't fully understand: when she left, like Natalie, she would be leaving forever.

Time ran out; she had to catch a train. In the end, she simply wrote what came into her mind: *If our paths never cross, you know I'm sorry. If I live to see the seven wonders, I'll make a path to the rainbow's end.* She signed it like he had on the flipside—with love.

Natalie slung the pack over her arm and across her back, and looked around Stevie's apartment. The walls were plastered with photos, all of the same woman. Natalie remembered that the woman was named Stevie Nicks. This was important, somehow. She loosened the tape behind one of the Stevie Nicks photos at her eye level. Nicks young, almost impossibly so, all smooth skin and brown eyes and frizzy, curly hair. In a three-quarter turn pose, she gripped the waist of her black tank top with manicured, ringed hands that, in comparison to her tiny waist, looked disproportionally, surprisingly—and to Natalie's eyes, comfortingly—huge and mannish. Natalie smoothed out the wrinkles from the picture.

Natalie Parsons' mission began now.

Author Biography

A literary and science fiction writer now based in Seattle, Romani writer Caren Gussoff grew up in Yonkers, NY. She received her MFA from the School of the Art Institute of Chicago. Before publishing her first novel, *Homecoming*, in 2000, Gussoff worked as a phone sex worker, apple cider press operator, a bar maid at raves, a high school science teacher, and a case worker for adolescent girls in foster care.

Gussoff was a finalist for the Village Voice's "Writers on the Verge" prize for *Homecoming*, and followed up with her second book, *The Wave and Other Stories,* in 2003. She then took a brief hiatus from writing, and worked as a burlesque revival performer, and taught college literature and cultural studies, as well as creative writing. In 2007, Gussoff returned to writing, embracing her personal love of sci fi, as a lifelong geek, and attended the Clarion West writing workshop, as the Carl Brandon Society's Octavia E. Butler Scholar. Since then, she has been published in multiple anthologies and magazines, winning awards such as the Hedgebrook Elizabeth George Award, the Speculative Literature Foundation's Gulliver Grant, a stint as the Seattle Post-Intelligencer's Geek of the Week, and honors from the European Commission on Science and Society.

Her latest novel is *The Birthday Problem* (2014) from Pink Narcissus Press, and a new writing guide, *Creating a Sustainable Writing Practice*, will be released from Eastlake & Roanoke.

Gussoff is currently at work on a new novel, evidenced by the disarray in the home she shares with her husband, artist Chris Sumption, and their two cats, Molly Bloom and Paul Atreides.

Find her online at spitkitten.com.

Made in United States
North Haven, CT
17 March 2025